The Mission Adventure

D0835248

Crossway books by Joni Eareckson Tada
I'll Be with You Always
You've Got a Friend
The Incredible Discovery of Lindsey Renee

Joni Eareckson Tada and Steve Jensen
Tell Me the Promises
Tell Me the Truth

DARCY AND FRIENDS
The Amazing Secret
The Unforgettable Summer
The Meanest Teacher
The Mission Adventure

The
Mission Adventure

JONI EARECKSON TADA
STEVE JENSEN

CROSSWAY BOOKS • WHEATON, ILLINOIS
A DIVISION OF GOOD NEWS PUBLISHERS

The Mission Adventure

Copyright © 2001 by Joni Eareckson Tada and Steve Jensen

Published by Crossway Books
      a division of Good News Publishers
      1300 Crescent Street
      Wheaton, Illinois 60187

All rights reserved. No part of this publication may be reproduced, stored in a retrieval system, or transmitted in any form by any means, electronic, mechanical, photocopy, recording, or otherwise, without the prior permission of the publisher, except as provided by USA copyright law.

Cover design: Cindy Kiple

Cover illustration: Matthew Archambault

First printing 2001

Printed in the United States of America

Library of Congress Cataloging-in-Publication Data
Tada, Joni Eareckson.
   The mission adventure / Joni Eareckson Tada and Steve Jensen.
      p. cm. — (Darcy and Friends ; 4)
   Summary: Although being in a wheelchair will make the trip difficult, Darcy feels called to go with members of her church on a mission to Guatemala, where she and her sister help a deaf orphan.
   ISBN 1-58134-257-8 (tpb : alk. paper)
   [1. Christian life—Fiction.   2. Physically handicapped—Fiction.
3. Wheelchairs—Fiction.   4. Missionaries—Fiction.   5. Sisters—
Fiction.]   I. Jensen, Steve. II. Title.
PZ7.T116 Mi   2001
[Fic]—dc21   2001000337
                                                CIP

| 15 | 14 | 13 | 12 | 11 | 10 | 09 | 08 | 07 | 06 | 05 | 04 | 03 | 02 | 01 |
| 15 | 14 | 13 | 12 | 11 | 10 | 9 | 8 | 7 | 6 | 5 | 4 | 3 | 2 | 1 |

To John Wern
A man seeking God's heart
and spreading God's love around the world

One

I sat alone and still, watching Sunday morning unwrap itself in our backyard. Mist rose from the ground like a lazy wave, passing from left to right across the grass. Shadows formed as the first rays of light crept through the grove of pine trees and over the roof of the house. The coming of the sun was soon followed by a chorus of birds hidden in the trees, each one trying to out-sing the others.

Wearing a nightshirt and holding a bowl of cereal, I had parked myself on the deck to enjoy the morning before anyone else got up. It was a part of my daily routine, and I enjoyed every minute of it. It was quiet. It was beautiful. And I was alone.

Alone, that is, except for a blue jay who also claimed the deck as his territory. We had met twice before that week at about the same time. Perched on the railing, he would hop from one side of the deck to the other. He was suspicious of me, but he was either too hungry or too curious to leave. Several times I had thrown out a cornflake or two for him, but he never had the courage to come closer. He had simply cackled his protest at my presence and then continued his hopping.

This time was different. Rather than stay on the railing, he hopped down to the deck floor, as if expecting me to give him something again.

"All right, all right," I said. I tossed a flake onto the deck two feet in front of me. The jay inched closer and closer, all the while cocking his head at me, as if I were laying a trap and would jump out of my chair and attack him.

He didn't have to worry about that. With my legs paralyzed from my waist to my toes, I would have landed facedown and flat on the deck.

I studied him closely as he took short sideways hops toward me. His feathers were bright blue with white and black markings. His tail was the longest I'd ever seen on a blue jay. I found myself wishing for a camera. *Not to worry—I'll have this bird eating out of my hands in a couple weeks.* The jay bobbed his head up and down, looking at me, then at the cornflake, and then at me again. He kept doing this until he was within a couple of inches of the prize.

My moments as a bird trainer came to a sudden end when out of nowhere a small speckled sparrow flew onto the deck. It bravely stepped in front of the blue jay, snatched the cornflake in its beak, and then took off. The sparrow stopped for an instant on the railing while he got a better grip on the flake and then disappeared into the tree above us. It happened so quickly the jay had no time to fight off the little thief—let alone give a squawk of protest.

I tried to keep the jay's interest by tossing another cornflake, this time a soggy one from the bottom of my bowl, but the jay seemed just as angry at me as at the sparrow. As far as he was concerned, the sparrow and I had planned the whole thing just to tease him. "It really was for you," I pleaded. The jay cocked his head back, gave a nasty squawk, and flew away without the cornflake.

My disappointment turned to anger at the sparrow. I squinted at the tree, but the bird was nowhere in sight. He was no doubt enjoying his victory and the giant breakfast of seventeen fortified vitamins and iron!

It didn't take long for my anger to turn to admiration for the little bird. I remembered how often blue jays had chased away sparrows from our bird feeder in order to get the best seeds. The sparrows always got the leftovers, and they never got the admiration that jays received for their beautiful feathers.

Although I couldn't see the sparrow, I decided he deserved a shout of congratulations. "You did it! Way to go, kid!" My voice echoed against the trees.

"Darcy DeAngelis, who are you talking to?"

Startled, I spun around in my wheelchair to face my dad, who was standing over me with a cup of coffee and the morning paper. Our golden retriever, EJ, stood at his side wagging his tail.

"You scared me, Dad!" I scolded, holding my chest.

"Sorry. It's just that I'm not used to my daughter talking to a tree at 6:30 in the morning. A little odd, don't you think?"

"Well, yeah, but you see this bird deserved it." I motioned back to the tree. "He came swooping down to get the cornflake I had left for the blue jay." I looked at the soggy flake on the deck and realized that my story might not sound believable. I stopped and glanced at my dad to see if he wanted to hear more.

"Whatever you say, Darcy." He pulled over a lounge chair next to me. EJ collapsed in a heap beside it. As Dad leaned over to wipe off the dew from the chair, I saw the top of his head thinning a little in the middle and sporting some gray. *He's getting old! I can't have a dad that looks like a grandpa! He'll be 100 years old by the time I graduate from high school! He'll be hard of hearing and . . .*

Dad caught me in mid-thought as he sat down, his blue-gray eyes smiling at me. In an instant he was young again, no older than my memories of him from younger days. He wasn't a big guy like my friend Chip's dad, but he was in good shape from exercising. And he looked young from his constant smiling. He was a good dad, and I was glad he was mine.

"Darcy," he said as he pushed away the paper, "mind if we talk a bit?"

I shook my head no, glad for the company now.

"Your mom and I have been talking and have decided . . ."

My heart skipped. It sounded like some awful news or terrible decision was about to be dumped on me—like him getting fired or he and Mom getting a divorce.

Dad caught my anxious look, then smiled, and

squeezed my shoulder. He went on. "We've decided you'll be needing a new wheelchair pretty soon. You've been telling us your chair is getting tight for you, and we agree." Dad smacked my tire with his wadded newspaper and asked, "What d'ya think?"

I breathed a sigh of relief and smiled back. I had been having problems with my wheelchair. It was uncomfortable, and it looked like a wreck. The leather was faded and cracked in places. There were scratches on the metal parts. And the dozens of stickers I had put on the chair over the years were dirty and half torn.

"Are you sure, Dad?" I asked. As much as I needed a new chair, I wasn't so certain I would like the replacement. What if they got me a clunky hospital-type wheelchair? Even though this one was old, at least it had a sporty look to it—with open sides and small footrests. If I got a new one, I'd want it to be as cool-looking, if not more. "Wheelchairs like this one are expensive, aren't they?" I asked, trying to let my dad know what I was thinking.

He ignored my question and reached into his pocket. "We were thinking of something like this," he said as he handed me a brochure. I recognized the Swiftie logo on the cover. The company's wheelchairs were top-notch, and many wheelchair athletes used them. I flipped open the brochure and saw a photo of a streamlined, low-backed, slick-sided, shiny chair with angled-in wheels. It was a brand-new Swiftie Model D80—the coolest wheelchair I'd ever seen. I pressed the brochure to my chest, feeling a little like an adult drooling over a sleek, black Lexus.

"Wow, Dad!" I gave a long, low whistle. "I can't believe it. Are you really sure?"

"Sure, I'm sure. I'm getting a bonus next month for a special project I did at work, and I thought it ought to go toward this." He reached over and hugged me. "We love you, kid." I hugged him back, hard.

"Now remember," he said, pulling away and pushing my shoulders up straight, "this wheelchair is going to last you awhile. That means it'll be a little large when you first get it. But you'll grow into it."

I nodded. I was already picturing what I'd look like in my zippy new wheels and what I'd be able to do. I'd glide down hallways, a thin, narrow silhouette from the side. I'd cruise down sidewalks and do cool tricks, like super-long wheelies and double spins.

"And just think, EJ," I said as I tugged his ear, "you'll have a lot easier job when you pull me down the sidewalk." He just looked up at me with those big, happy eyes of his and then dropped his head back onto the deck.

"Well," Dad said, as he took a last sip of coffee and got up from his chair, "I've got to get ready for church. Don't stay out too long. We leave in an hour, and I don't want us to be late."

"Right." I gave a thumbs-up. "And, Dad . . ."

"Yeah?"

"Thanks again."

I flipped through the brochure after he went back into the house. My eyes jumped from picture to picture and then focused on phrases such as "latest technology" and "lightweight titanium bearings." The birds in the trees chattered more loudly as the rays of the sun filled and warmed the backyard. The beauty of the morning was lost on me now as I daydreamed about my new wheelchair.

✣ ✣ ✣

My perfect morning continued later on at church. The same bright sun filtered through the tall windows, making the sanctuary bright and airy while the piano played something soft and pretty. I was glad that Dad and Mom always tried to get us to church early. It made me feel a little more prepared and a lot less rushed.

I sat next to my sister Monica in the pew. She had helped me transfer out of the wheelchair and onto the velvet cushion on the pew bench so I could feel more like I was at church. The other kids complained about how the pew made their backsides hurt. Not me. I didn't feel a thing!

As I listened to the music, I thought about how unusual it would have been to sit next to Monica a year ago. She would have hung out with her high school friends on the other side of the sanctuary. I was glad that during the past few months she and I had grown closer. For some reason she no longer seemed like the airhead she used to be. And she had told me that I no longer seemed like a spoiled brat to her. We were more like friends, true friends, than sisters.

A warm feeling flooded my heart, and I stole a sideways glance at Monica. I found myself wishing I could be more like her. She was popular, a cheerleader, a member of student government, and she played the lead in her school's production of *Showboat*. She was one of those do-everything-well types who gets voted for everything by everyone. Monica was active in the youth group at church, always organizing special events and acting on the drama team. Grades were never a problem for her.

Here I felt good about myself. I could always keep up with her in the brains department, but I fell short when it came to the "my hair has so much bounce and shine" stuff. I felt a twinge of jealousy at Monica's good looks. My mind went back to a conversation between us about a year ago.

"You know, Darcy," she had said, "I had the same problem of looking like a stupid dork in junior high, but you'll grow out of it."

I had stormed out of the room in anger. But now as I thought about it, it seemed a nice, sisterly thing for her to say. However, I knew my eyebrows would always be wiry, my eyelashes too thin, my freckles too big, and my hair always at war with my brush and comb. A "Monica" I was not. But that was okay. It felt good being Monica's sister and sitting together at church.

I spotted my best friends, Chip and Mandy, in the pew behind us. I began thinking about some of the ups and downs we had shared during seventh grade. *I'm glad that's behind us.*

We'd all be eighth graders at Jordan Junior High in the fall. In fact, now that I'd gotten used to junior high,

I was beginning to enjoy school. Whether it was pop quizzes from Mr. Dempsey, our journalism teacher, or gathering up wet towels after the showers at P.E., it was all part of what school was supposed to be. It felt good to me to fit into class routines.

The world of junior high, like everything else in my life, seemed perfect. My circle of friends was just the right size. No one noticed my disability anymore, and I felt better about myself. Kids were used to my wheelchair in the hallways, and nobody gave me a hard time if they had to step aside to keep their toes from getting run over. Besides, nothing felt neater than to wheel at high speed toward a friend in the hallway and slap a "high five" in passing. Even my clothes that felt so loose at the beginning of the school year now fit just right. And words came a lot easier to me when I hung out with kids in the lobby before homeroom bell or stood in line at the cafeteria.

Thoughts of school gave way to the scene around me as the pianist began a different hymn. The wooden pews and the deep red carpet made the church look like the inside of a king's castle. The light pouring through the windows had shifted and now washed the cross on the wall behind the Communion table with a golden glow. Large circular fans way up high in the ceiling moved the air around in a nice breeze, making it feel as if we were outside.

I had begun to enjoy my church more and more lately too. And it wasn't just the building. Our youth pastor really cared about us, and he always planned the coolest things—pizza party sleepovers in the church basement, game nights, scavenger hunts, and Friday night campfires down by Willowbrook Lake. Besides all that, just being with everyone at church made the place feel special, like Jesus was actually there.

As the ushers passed the offering plate up and down the aisles, I checked off in my mind all the things about my world that seemed just right. The piano played in the background while I closed my eyes. I imagined my life all laid out like a big blueprint, every-thing neat and tidy and fitting together. The blueprint had places for my new wheelchair, our house, my friends, my school, my dog, my sister—all of it con-necting together.

I wanted life to stay like this forever. But little did I realize that within just a few minutes, while I was sit-ting there in the church pew near front and center, God would turn my perfect world upside down.

Two

It was Pastor Rob's announcement that started it all. The offering had just been taken when he stepped up to the pulpit microphone.

"We have a special treat for you this morning," he began. "You might remember that we prayed about a small church in Guatemala during missions week last October. Now through God's guidance we're pleased to have the pastor of that church and his family with us this morning. Pastor Zepeda, would you come up here on the platform and bring your beautiful family with you?"

A short, dark-haired man stood up. His wife and four children also shuffled out of the pew and made their way up the aisle to the platform. I watched closely. One of the girls seemed to be my age; the rest of the kids were younger. They seemed nervous as if they were animals in a zoo being stared at. Their clothing, though clean, was out of date and mismatched. When they paused behind the pulpit, the entire family huddled close to each other and smiled nervously at the people.

"Pastor Zepeda is going to share a few words about his church. Pastor, please come and tell us what's on your heart."

The pastor stepped forward and shook Pastor Rob's hand. His family gathered close behind him.

"Thank you," he said with an accent as he adjusted the microphone. "We are happy to be here. I bring greetings from your brothers and sisters in Christ in Guatemala. My family and I live in a town called Gomera, about two or three hours southwest of the capital city. Though there are not many of us in our church in Gomera, we share the love of Christ with our neighbors."

He read stiffly from his notes, looking up only once, as if to see if we were still there. He didn't have to worry. I looked over my shoulder at Mandy and Chip, and, like me, they were hanging on every word.

Maybe it was the pastor's odd clothes or his accent, or maybe he and his family looked like somebody on the Discovery channel. Whatever it was, we were all fascinated. This man and this moment both seemed special. He told us about his church, the conditions in Guatemala, and the hopes they had for the future.

"I have pictures to show you," he said.

Pastor Rob came to the microphone. "That's right, folks. Jim Wilcox of our missions committee took them last month when he and I visited Pastor Zepeda's church. Ushers, would you turn out the lights?"

Clicking to the first slide, Pastor Zepeda stepped back and said with pride, "This is our church."

I didn't believe it at first. The building had at one time been painted pink, but now only faded clay bricks showed through. There were a couple of concrete slabs outside the doorway. I squinted and could tell that there was no floor inside—just hard dirt. It was like the dirt street outside. There was no sign near the door. No parking places. No grass. No flowers, except for a few colorful blossoms that clung to a scraggly bush at the corner. Only the cross attached to the roof gave any clear sign that it was a church.

Slide after slide, Pastor Zepeda showed us what life was like in his town. The people who owned the shops. A neighbor who tended goats. A few women weaving baskets. Some kids riding a burro. He even showed a few slides of some people living in the streets. I especially noticed in one slide that a couple of the people were sitting all bent over, as if their legs were twisted. Something about them hit home. Then I realized, *They're disabled . . . like me!*

He clicked to the next slide of a hospital, but it looked more like a jail. It was awful. But as I watched Pastor Zepeda's daughters smile at the slides, I could tell that they thought it was anything but awful. To them it was home. That made me feel better about seeing the dirt streets and rundown buildings. I could tell that Pastor Zepeda loved the people in his town and was glad to be a pastor. I sat there thinking that if I were God, I would be very pleased with the Zepeda family.

The lights came back on when the slides were done. Some people rubbed their eyes from the brightness, and others seemed to be wiping away tears. I glanced over my shoulder at Mandy, who mouthed a silent "Wow!" Everyone was quiet as Mr. Wilcox stepped up, shook the hand of the pastor, and then turned to the congregation.

"The missions committee has a special announcement and an invitation. You've heard from Pastor

Zepeda about his church and have seen firsthand the needs there. The opportunities in his town are tremendous, and we are going to have a part in helping his people. Pastor Zepeda has invited us to come to Guatemala. We're going to partner with the people in his church and do some exciting things in his town. First, we're going to distribute tracts and Bibles. We're also going to bring materials and paint to help fix up the church building. Those of you handy with hammers and saws will no doubt want to work on this project. We'll also take medical supplies with us like medicine, wheelchairs, bandages . . ."

Mr. Wilcox continued, but my mind had frozen on one word.

Wheelchairs!

They were going to deliver wheelchairs. I remembered the slide of those disabled people who lined the street and wondered how they got around. Now I knew. They didn't get around. They didn't have any wheelchairs.

"The trip is being scheduled for July 6-16. We'd like all of you to go home and pray about going on this trip. It'll require time and money on your part. And don't think of this as a vacation. Conditions, food, and customs will be different from what you're used to."

Mr. Wilcox stepped aside for Pastor Rob. "Come next to me, Pastor Zepeda, won't you? And bring your family with you. Let's pray."

We bowed our heads as Pastor Rob prayed for the Zepeda family.

"Please, Lord, give Your servants in Guatemala special courage. Be with this man's family and his church. And may many from our church make it their mission to go on this trip. In Jesus' name, amen."

We opened our eyes. I watched the Zepeda family leave the platform. And at that moment I felt as though God had begun making big changes in my life. But it was more than that, more than something He would do on the outside. Something changed inside me. I don't know if you can ever tell when you decide you've grown up, but at that moment I knew. I didn't think like a kid anymore. I prayed silently at that moment of discovery, *I want to go too, Lord.*

❊ ❊ ❊

I gave my reasons for going to Guatemala to my folks around the dinner table after church. "Please, Mom, you're always talking about how I need to learn responsibility, and this trip would be great for that!"

My new sense of growing up was real, but no one else seemed to realize that. My family needed convincing. "Learn responsibility" was a good phrase to use to show them.

"I have to admit, Darcy," my dad said, "that the slides showed a lot of needs there, and Pastor Zepeda certainly needs help. But what makes you think you should be the one to go?"

"Because I just know, Dad. I mean, I really prayed about it the whole time Pastor Rob was speaking."

My dad smiled. "Okay, let's assume you should go. There are some things that get in the way though, aren't there?"

"Like what?" I challenged him. I couldn't imagine any problems, and if there were, I was ready to tackle them. I gripped my fork tightly, ready to stab at his arguments like the pieces of roast beef on my plate.

"Well, first, there's the question of money. The airfare alone will be a lot, I'm sure."

"A gazillion dollars!" my little brother Josh shouted.

"It is not, Josh, and keep out of this," I said not too nicely.

Dad was probably right. I had ignored the costs, thinking I could live on candy bars and crackers I would stuff in my suitcase. But I hadn't counted on airline tickets.

"Where would you get the money?" Mom asked.

My mind raced through ideas—baby-sitting, cleaning, even selling some of my stuff. But I knew it probably wouldn't be enough. My face showed the disappointment.

"Fund-raisers!" Monica blurted out. "You and others going on the trip could raise money with car washes and bake sales and stuff." Mom and Dad looked at Monica as if to say "mind your own business."

"Just a thought," she sighed and shrugged her shoulders.

"And it's a good one, sis," I said, feeling encouraged that she was on my side. "Monica's right. Kids do it all the time. And maybe I could raise, you know, uh, support from people who could sponsor me, kind of like what missionaries do."

Mom and Dad looked at each other. They weren't convinced.

"Let's just say I had the money. Could I go then?"

"The money isn't the only thing, Darcy. You're still forgetting one thing. How are you going to get along down there on your own? You can't expect the others to help with all your morning and evening exercises and bath and stuff. There are a lot of things you can do, but two weeks in another country is a long time. You'd need a lot of help."

Mom and Dad said that last part with some hesitation. It was one of those "disability things" that often made a task for me more difficult than for other kids my age. I could tell my parents felt bad about bringing it up.

Mom cleared her throat and said, "Don't you agree that you'll need someone to go with you? And neither your dad nor I can go."

This was definitely a brick wall that seemed impossible to get through. No matter how much money I raised, it wouldn't solve this problem. As much as I hated to admit it, my parents were right. From the looks of those slides, I'd need someone to push me around. And, of course, who knew what kind of bathtubs or showers there would be? And what about bathrooms? Could I even get into one to use the toilet?

Then Monica—my wonderful, perfect, too-good-to-be-true sister—came to my rescue. "I'll go," she piped up. "I'll help Darcy."

I was dumbstruck. Mom's mouth dropped. Dad raised his eyebrows. Even Josh chuckled when EJ seemed to whine on cue from underneath the table. A moment of silence fell around the table until Dad recovered.

"But you're going to college in the fall, Monica," he said.

"I know. But that's not till the end of summer."

"But your life-guarding job—wasn't that to make money for college?"

"I can probably make arrangements for a couple of weeks . . . I think. It's not like I'd be giving up all that much money. Besides, I've got those scholarships. And, Dad, I really felt moved to do something too after church this morning. It's like Darcy says, I feel like God has a special plan for this trip, and I want to be a part of it. Do you know what I mean?"

"I admit I do," Dad said. "Your mom and I felt that way too when we were young. We traveled to Indonesia before any of you were born. It was one of the best things we've ever done."

Mom and Dad looked at each other. That last comment of his gave me hope.

"Do you remember the time we shared Christ with those people on that street corner who didn't understand a word we were saying?" Dad chuckled. Mom nodded her head. "We'd have been stuck without those Bibles."

My parents had that faraway look on their faces, remembering something that obviously meant a lot to them.

"You're starting to convince us, Darcy," Dad said. "Look at us—you've got your mother and me wanting to pack for Guatemala ourselves. Tell you what. Let's pray about it tonight. Then give us a little more time to talk it over. We'll need to see how God provides for each step of the way—money, Monica's schedule, visas, and permission from the church."

"This is incredible! This is great! And it's a deal," I said, with a slap on the table. I knew that things such as permissions and schedules could present problems later on, but I was convinced that God would easily tackle them. My perfect world was now being changed, and I was glad. Perfection is just a little boring.

Later that night I wheeled into Monica's room. I wanted to tell her a big "thanks." I paused in the doorway and watched her listening to music and writing a letter. She lay in bed, stationery and address cards spread out all over the covers.

"Who are you writing to?" I asked.

"Some friends I met at the retreat last winter. I'm telling them about our trip to Pastor Zepeda's church."

"Not so fast, Monica. We're not going yet. Mom and Dad only said they would pray about it."

"I know. But didn't you see the look in their eyes when they talked about *their* mission trip. It's a sure thing. You'll see."

"I hope so," I sighed with a smile.

I moved my wheelchair closer. "There's one thing I don't understand though, Monica. Why did you volunteer to go—and especially to go and help me? I mean, you've been a great sister and all, but getting me in and out of the bathroom has never been your favorite thing. You once said you'd rather give a bath to a rhinoceros. And why a missions trip to Guatemala, of all things? Did you see those slides, Monica? There isn't a hair dryer in sight."

She laughed at my teasing. She was a stickler for looking good, and it was obvious the trip would be a disaster for the glamour department.

"Yeah, I know, but listen. I realized today while sitting in church that we don't have a lot of time left together. This trip would be kind of like a going-away thing. One last fling as sisters before I move out for college. You know what I mean?"

Monica, for all her maturity, seemed suddenly awkward, like she had said something dumb or embarrassing. But she hadn't. Monica was feeling the same thing I felt.

"I do," I said, slowly wheeling closer to her bed.

"I'm going off to college, and my life's going to change, Darcy. I won't be back here except for vacations." She sat on the edge of the bed and put her hands on my shoulders. "This is it, kiddo. We may not get another chance to do sister stuff like this again."

I looked up at my sister. Her eyes were soft, and her smile was warm. My eyes welled up with tears, and my bottom lip quivered. The thought of saying goodbye overwhelmed me. Another part of my life was about to change. My perfect world would be shattered in a few months, just as my sister and I were beginning to get our family act together. Up until this moment, the thought of a big change in my life seemed challenging, even exciting. But now feelings of fear and worry began to creep in.

Three

I was glad to shut the door of my own bedroom that night just so I could be alone with all my confused thoughts. One minute I was full of hope; the next minute I was battling fear. The painful thought of Monica's leaving for college kept clashing with the excitement of going to Guatemala. Both feelings kept me awake in bed for the longest time. I finally turned on the bedside lamp and reached in the top drawer of the nightstand for my Box.

My Box was my quiet friend, and in it I stuffed all my letters—mostly letters I had written to myself. Seeing my feelings on paper helped me to think straight. Other times it gave me a chance to let off steam about something without anyone knowing. I flipped through the letters and reread some old ones about Chip, my almost-but-not-quite boyfriend, who was really my best friend. I couldn't reveal it to anyone but Mandy, because most people would think I had the "weirds" for him. Reading about Chip made me smile. I flipped to another page and read about the time I discovered that EJ had a strange and painful hip disease. I sighed and touched an old mark on the page that I recognized as a tearstain.

At times my Box made me laugh. Other times it let me cry. Sometimes, like tonight, it was my place to pray. I reached for a pen and began writing my prayer.

Lord, I can't get to sleep. I'm mixed up about my feelings. I think I know why. We all promised each other we'd pray about this tonight, and though I've spent a lot of time thinking about the trip, I haven't really prayed about it.

You know that I want to go. Now I need to know if You want me to go. It's such a big chance, Lord. I'd be a terrific missionary—don't You think? I mean, I'm in a wheelchair, and

we're taking wheelchairs down there! I could
show them the same love I got from You.

"Oh, great," I said, as I flipped my pen in the air
and rolled my eyes. I realized that although I was taking Spanish in school, I'd have a hard time being a missionary in a Spanish-speaking country. I started praying
out loud: "I'm glad I'm taking Spanish in school, Lord.
But You know my grades aren't so good. So please, if I
do go to Guatemala, would You help me get a good
grade in Spanish too?"

I laughed at myself. Sometimes it was so much
fun talking to God. I never felt that He thought I asked
dumb stuff even when I was going overboard, like asking for a good grade in Spanish so I could speak to
people in a strange country I wasn't even sure I was
going to.

I pictured myself talking to a group of people in
Guatemala. I'd be on a platform looking out over a sea
of faces—all of the people in brand-new wheelchairs.
I'd share about Jesus in Spanish, getting all my verbs
just right, and when I asked how many would like to
invite Him into their hearts, dozens of hands would
raise. I replayed that scene several times in my mind
before continuing to write.

Lord, You know how wonderful it would be to tell all those people about You. Please let me know if You'd like it too.

I signed my name, wrote the date at the bottom, folded the letter, and closed the lid on the Box. Turning off the lamp, I lay again in the darkness. I felt a sense of peace. I had asked God in faith and knew that He'd do the best thing. Before long my eyes felt heavy, and I drifted off to sleep.

The next morning Dad asked everyone to have breakfast together. Something like that usually only happens at Christmas. At first I thought it was odd, but then it made sense: Monica and I, and even Josh, knew that the discussion about Guatemala was only half-finished. The showers ran, doors slammed, and hair dryers whined, after which Monica and I were downstairs in record time.

"Okay, gang," Dad announced at the head of the breakfast table, "your mother and I prayed about the trip to Guatemala last night."

"You're going too?" Josh interrupted as he slid into his seat late. "What about me?"

"No, no, we're not going. And neither are you, Josh. But Darcy and Monica might. Listen to this verse Mom and I came across last night." Dad opened up his Bible as he took a sip of coffee. "It says, 'Trust in the Lord with all your heart, and don't lean on your own understanding. In all your ways acknowledge Him, and He will make your paths straight.' That's Proverbs 3:5 and 6."

I smiled inside. That's what I had sensed last night as I prayed. I was really leaving it up to God. I knew I wanted to go, but I had a feeling I couldn't push too hard. No more Darcy plotting to make something go her way. This time it was up to God.

"So how do we do that, guys?" Mom asked.

"Well," Monica said, "there are a lot of things we don't know yet or don't have, just like Dad said last night. We don't have the money, we don't know if I can find a replacement lifeguard, and we don't even know if Darcy would be allowed to go."

"What do you mean?" I asked.

Monica folded her arms and explained, "Well, Darcy, we know you're superwoman and everything, but maybe the missions committee or the people in Guatemala will put up a barrier. They might not want you to go because of, you know, because of your disability."

I shoved my plate aside and visibly pouted.

"Hey, come on," Mom encouraged me. "We've

gone through this sort of stuff before, Darcy. You've got to get used to people doubting your abilities. Many people put up roadblocks in your path, but don't assume everyone will. Like Monica says, let's just put it on our list of things we need to rely on God for."

"I guess so." I was a little discouraged. "Anything else we're going to put on the list?"

"Well, there are always things like getting passports and visas and inoculations," Dad said.

I couldn't believe this was my dad talking. Just last night he was sending out a lot of "no" signals. Now he was honestly adding things to the list to be prayed about, as if he really wanted me to go.

"So, Dad," I said, "you and Mom are saying we can go, right?"

They smiled and Dad said, "Well, of course, we're saying it's okay. But let me ask both of you—did you pray about it?"

Monica nodded. We knew this wasn't another of Dad's spiritual lectures. It was kind of a family agreement that we all had to depend on God to make this happen. "I prayed too," I piped up. "It wasn't like I saw a big neon sign come flashing on, but I felt kind of like . . ."

"Like everything was going to be okay?" Monica interrupted.

"Yeah," I agreed. "That's right. How did you know?"

"'Cause I felt the same way," she said softly.

Right there around the breakfast table, our entire family knew that God had at that instant provided all the encouragement we needed. He would find a way for us to go. Dad clapped his hands and concluded, "Okay, it's settled. Now let's get working on our 'To Do and Believe List' and see how God directs."

❊ ❊ ❊

It was one of those "why-am-I-here" days at school. Going to Guatemala made homeroom announcements seem twice as boring. All the way to school I had day-dreamed about the trip and about what I had to do to prepare. My homeroom classmates were all excited for me and asked me zillions of questions, to which I had no answers. I looked at the calendar on the wall and felt as if I were in prison, being forced to count the days before my release.

It wasn't until I got to social studies class that I suddenly realized school need not be a prison after all. Mr. Dawson reminded us about our end-of-the-year project—a big report on some foreign country. Last week I had chosen Chile for my project, but suddenly

I hit upon a brilliant idea. *I know—I'm going to do my final project on Guatemala!*

I pleaded with Mr. Dawson, "Please, can I write about Guatemala? You see, I'm making plans to go there in July, and it would give me a chance to learn all about the geography and the people and the culture and stuff."

Mr. Dawson shuffled his papers and shook his head. "I don't know, Darcy. You don't have much time before school is over."

"Oh, please. Hardly anyone has started theirs anyway. And, besides, you always talk about what we study being relevant to everyday life. What better way is there to prove it?"

I'd used the big word *relevant* to clinch my case. It showed I was listening. It showed I was learning. Actually it showed I was a good saleswoman.

"Okay, okay, you got me. Go ahead and change it. But don't say I didn't warn you if your report is late because you run out of time."

"No sweat!" I answered.

As with history class, Spanish took on a whole new meaning that day. It was no longer a boring waste of time. Everything made sense. I hung on every word the teacher said. The best I'd ever done in Spanish was a B. The rest of my grades were C's and D's. I was determined to change that, and I knew I could.

I thought school would be a drag, since my mind was on the upcoming trip, but I was wrong. I began learning in a whole new way. I even thought of how I could make pre-algebra fit into the trip somewhere. Maybe I'd need to calculate something for the construction crew.

Mom picked me up outside of school that afternoon. She was all smiles as she stood outside the car, waiting for me. *She's so pretty when she smiles like that.* It was one of those moments when I wanted everyone to know she was my mom, and I wanted to be like her.

I wheeled up to the car.

"Hi, Mom," I greeted her.

"I've got good news, Darcy," she said. "I spoke with Mr. Wilcox at his office today. He thinks it'd be wonderful if you could go on the trip to Guatemala!"

"Really?"

"Yes. And that's not all. He said, 'You know, if Darcy is coming with us, she could be of real help when we give out those wheelchairs. There will be people who have never used one before, and maybe Darcy could teach them. She would be our wheelchair specialist.' Now what do you think of that?"

"Specialist! He said I could be a specialist?" I sort of knew what the word meant. There were doctors I had that were called specialists—surgeons and radiologists and people like that. Now I was a specialist!

"There's one thing though," my mom said. "The trip won't be cheap. It'll cost about $1,000 per person."

"$1,000!" It knocked the wind out of me. "It might as well be a million!"

"Now don't get discouraged," she said. "Remember—God will direct our paths."

Though I was overwhelmed with how much money I would need to raise, my excitement still grew that afternoon. Monica came home with checkpoint #2 on our "To Do and Believe" list taken care of.

"It was totally awesome!" she said as she burst through the door. "I hadn't even told anyone about my trip because I wanted to be sure I could get time off from work. Well, here I am in line at lunch when Frank Cooper comes up to me. He and I hardly ever talk 'cause he's a junior, and one time he totally grossed me out with—"

"Get to the point, Monica," I said.

"Okay, okay, anyway he says—you won't believe this . . ."

"I believe it! I believe it!" I yelled impatiently. "What did he say?"

"He said, 'Monica, I know you'll probably say no, but if you ever get sick or something during the summer, and they need someone to take your place for a couple of days, could you please put in a word for me. I really need life-guarding experience, and there aren't any jobs open for the summer.'"

"I could have died on the spot. Anyway I didn't overreact or get too excited. I just said, 'Well, as a matter of fact, I'm needing a couple of weeks off in July. Could you do it for that long?' He almost dropped his books, he was so excited. I made him promise. I said, 'If you back out, so help me, you'll never see your teeth again.'"

"Monica!"

"Oh, Mom, I was only teasing him. Anyway I called the pool manager before I left school and checked with him. He said, 'No sweat.' Isn't that great?"

"Yeah. That's two down," I said.

"Two?"

"Mr. Wilcox said I can go." I told Monica about the specialist part. We laughed and hooted like guys watching the Super Bowl. We replayed everything that everyone had said that day, several times.

When our enthusiasm quieted down, Monica brought up the big one. "What about the money? How much will it cost?"

"A lot," I said. "Mom told me Mr. Wilcox said it would cost around $1,000. Per person!"

"Per person?"

"That's what I said. Where are we going to get that kind of money? I don't have it. And you need to save the money you've got for college," I reminded her.

"Well, we've got some time. Let's come up with some ideas on how we can raise the money." We moved our conversation from the kitchen into the family room where Monica picked up a pen and pad of paper.

"There's always baby-sitting," I offered.

"Check!" Monica wrote the idea down on the paper. "I can do about three or four nights a week. Maybe you can find some afternoon jobs."

"And we can throw allowances into the pot now and then. And there are car washes," I continued. "Maybe the youth group can help us. Like maybe some of the others want to go."

"And we could do other fund-raisers, like writing letters and doing speeches and stuff. You know, like you said last night."

"I guess so. But don't ask me to stand up and ask

for money." I shuddered at the thought of doing that, and the idea sent a dark cloud over everything else we had thought of. "This seems impossible, Monica. There's got to be something we can do that will raise money."

Monica sat on the floor, her head in her hands, looking off somewhere. A simple smile came to her face. "There is, Darcy. We can pray. This is impossible. That's why it'll be exciting to see how God will do it."

"Yeah, you're right. Can we pray right now?"

We bowed our heads and prayed together. My heart was warm with joy. There wasn't any parent or Sunday school teacher or pastor around to lead us—just two sisters deciding on their own that they needed to pray together.

* * *

The next two months were full of ups and downs. The letters in my Box read as if different people were writing them. One day I'd be high as a bird—when we got our passports from the government. The next day I'd be down in the dumps—when two baby-sitting jobs fell through.

May 24th. Got my passport in the mail today. The picture looks dorky, but the passport is so cool. It's got special designs on it, and it looks like something a spy would have. I took it to school and showed my friends.

May 25th. The McGuire family canceled the baby-sitting job today. And the Barrets canceled for Friday night. So I'm still $833 away from my goal!

May 29th. Found a neat book at the library on Guatemala. The country is so interesting but sometimes sad. There are two types of people there—Indians and Spanish. Most people speak Spanish, but many still speak native Indian. The people are poor. The average person earns $100 a month. Half the people can't read or write. And there are lots of street kids— orphans who live on their own.

June 6th. The youth group did a car wash to raise money for us. Three others in the group are going too. The total came to $495, so each one going gets $99! Now I've got $734 left to raise. Please, Lord, it's just a month away.

June 10th. The church has been having a wheelchair drive. So far we've collected more than fifty chairs to take with us. We spent the day washing them. Lots of them have been up in attics collecting dust. Mr. Wilcox says that the chairs would cost someone in Guatemala a lot of money. They'd have to work for a year and spend all the money on just the chair. I thought about my wheelchair. Dad is getting me a new one with his bonus from work. I wonder how much it is actually going to cost.

June 15th. There's one week left before we have to have all our money raised. Dad and Mom are encouraging, but we're all anxious. Monica is $280 short, and I'm $460 short. Mom and Dad have already given toward our goal. They offered to help out more today, but we said no— we'd find a way.

❄ ❄ ❄

The week to raise the last amount of money went faster than I wanted it to. We got another $150 from relatives on Friday who had heard about our trip. That left $590 to raise between the two of us. Saturday was Slave Day. We hired ourselves out to people who, instead of paying us, gave a contribution toward our trip. By day's end, after slaving over weedy flower beds, washing windows (I did the bottom half, Monica the top), and cleaning out garages, we had raised just $120.

"Just $470 left to raise between the two of us, Darcy," Monica said. She was trying to smile and encourage me, but I was not in the mood. I started to cry.

"Why would we get this far, only to miss our chance of going? It's not fair!" I said the words before I thought. It was my usual response to things when they didn't go my way. I had trusted God to guide our way, but I wasn't happy with where He had led us.

Monica urged, "Cheer up, Darcy. It's not Sunday yet. We still have until tomorrow after church. Remember, we're just trusting God on this one. Whatever He decides is best, right?"

"Yeah, I guess. But if He wasn't going to get us the money, I wish He'd get it over with."

Our time around the supper table was quiet except for the usual, "Pass the peas," or "Sit up straight, Josh." The silence was killing me. Everyone felt uncomfortable.

It was Dad who finally spoke. "Darcy, I know you two have been working hard on raising money. Mom and I admire you not wanting to get any more money from us, so I had this idea."

Dad pushed his food around his plate. Whatever he was going to say seemed serious.

"If you really want to go on the trip, you might consider this idea. The wheelchair we're getting you is what you've wanted, but there are others that are cheaper. We could . . . well, you know, buy the ProWheel, for example, instead of the MD80. It would save about $500. We could give the money we save toward your trip."

I held my glass in midair and looked around the table. Monica was staring at me. Josh looked back and forth at Dad and me. My face flushed. I couldn't believe what Dad had just said. And I didn't know what to answer. Though Guatemala had filled my thoughts recently, hardly a day went by that I didn't daydream about the new chair. Some nights I had taken out the brochure and looked at it while lying in bed. Now Dad was about to ruin it all.

"But, Dad," I began to complain.

"Wait, Darcy. Before you get upset or argue, I'm not telling you that you have to. I am only giving you the option. It's your choice."

I felt numb. I also felt the pressure. I know Dad didn't mean to, but he had put me on the spot. It was up to me to get us to Guatemala. I don't remember finishing my supper. I only remember feeling hurt and wanting to be alone. *Life is hard enough in this chair. Just once I'd like to have something nice for myself. Why did Dad have to go and ruin it?*

The remainder of supper was even more silent. Even Josh kept still. It wasn't until we were all finished and clearing the table that Mom broke the ice. "Hey, why don't we all go out for ice cream. It's gotten so serious here, and maybe we just need to get out and have fun for a bit. What do you think?" She looked at Dad and then at the rest of us, resting her eyes on me.

I looked back at her briefly but said nothing. Josh shouted, "Yeah!" and ran into the garage.

Monica nodded with a small smile and looked at me. "C'mon, Darcy, it'll take our minds off things for a while."

"I think I'll stay home," I answered. "You guys can go."

"But, Darcy, let's be together tonight. I mean we're all feeling kinda down, and we need to cheer each other up."

"I know, but you guys can go and bring your ice cream back here. It's a nuisance with the van and all." I wasn't lying. Sometimes I hated how long it took for us to go places simply because I was in my wheelchair. Sometimes it was easier not to do anything or go anywhere. I convinced my family that I'd be all right. It felt good to be angry. I wanted to make Dad feel bad for the spot he had put me in.

I watched the car pull out of the garage and head down the street. I turned back to the kitchen, thought about doing the dishes, but changed my mind and went out onto the deck. *I hope they're gone a long time.*

The sun was still bright in the sky, although it was lower and covered by the trees. I closed my eyes and listened to the wind sway the branches. Dad had mowed the grass that day, and several rabbits came out to enjoy the clover. Birds sang in the trees around me.

As I was looking out over the yard, from the corner of my eye I saw something move. I turned my head and saw him there. It was a sparrow, maybe the same sparrow that had stolen the cornflake from the blue jay that Sunday morning. His wings twitched, and his head jerked in all directions as he looked for something.

"Sorry, not tonight," I said. "I haven't got a thing. In fact, I need some things myself. Got $470 on you?"

The bird seemed to like the sound of my voice. He hopped closer to me.

"Brave little guy, aren't you," I said. He hopped closer still. I was amazed. It's not like he didn't know I was there. I finally sat still and didn't say another word.

♉

He stopped next to my left tire. There, stuck between two spokes of my left wheel, was a french fry from supper. The sparrow quickly grabbed it in his beak, and as soon as he had a tight grip, flew up into the tree above me.

I looked up at the bird. It was then that my anger melted in me. I thought about that plain, small bird. I knew God took care of him, just as He did all the other birds. The sparrow was satisfied to look the way he did. He didn't have pretty blue feathers, and yet he seemed to do just fine.

The more I thought of it, the more I realized what God wanted. And it was what I wanted too. I really cared about the people in Guatemala, even if I hadn't met them. I'd be a hypocrite if I had to have the best wheelchair while knowing there were people who didn't have any wheelchair at all. "Thanks," I said out loud to the bird and to the sky.

Within a few minutes I heard the garage door open and the sound of our van's engine. My heart was skipping with nervousness. I wanted to tell my family my decision, but I felt awkward about how I'd do it.

"Here you go, Darcy," Mom said as she came out onto the deck first. "I picked up a praline twist for you. Thought you might have changed your mind about ice cream. Everything okay here?"

"Sure," I said softly. After everyone was out on the deck and seated, licking at the last part of their cones, I announced my decision. "I thought about your idea, Dad," I said. Everyone stopped eating, except for Josh. "I'd like to get the ProWheel. And could you use the difference for our trip, like you said?"

Dad looked at me for a long time and then smiled and nodded his head. "That would be fine, Darcy. If that's what you want to do."

"It is. Really. I decided."

"What changed your mind, Darcy? I mean, even though you didn't say anything at supper, I could tell you were pretty set on that other chair. Why the sudden change?" Monica asked.

I thought for a minute. "Oh, you could say a little bird told me." No one understood my humor, and I didn't explain.

We sat together on the deck quietly, finishing our ice cream and enjoying the sunset. Finally Josh couldn't stand the silence any longer. "So does that mean you're going to Guatemala?" he asked.

Looking at Monica with a wide smile and then at Josh, I said, "*Sí, señor.* We're on our way!"

Four

Once we knew for sure that we were going to Guatemala, the rest of our days before the trip went quickly. The end of school kept me busy with tests, parties, cleaning out my locker, and finishing up art projects. My new wheelchair came the day before school ended, giving me time to show it off a bit. The chair, though not the MD80 model with the super-slick, customized features, meant more to me because it enabled me to go to Guatemala. Arriving when it did allowed my old chair to be included in the supply of wheelchairs we'd take to Central America!

With all these activities to fill up the days, it wasn't long before we found ourselves curbside at the airport, checking in our luggage. We grabbed some chewing gum and a couple of magazines from the airport gift shop and made our way to the gate. We had fifteen minutes to boarding time. We joined the group of twenty-five other people from our church waiting at the right of the jetway.

"Now are you sure you've got everything?" Mom asked.

"Of course, Mom. We packed everything together, you and me, remember?" I could tell she was nervous and was trying to be my mom up to the last minute.

"Monica, be sure to be extra careful with hygiene for Darcy. Remember, the conditions are rough, and the water can be 'iffy.' We can't have her coming down with infections on the trip."

"Mom!" I was so embarrassed. I hoped no one heard my mother talking about Monica helping me with my bath. Mom just smiled at my protest. She would have continued with her long checklist, but Dad interrupted.

"Both of you are going to have to work as a team when it comes to transportation. You've got to transfer to another plane in Miami, and you've only got forty minutes to do so. And keep a good tight grip on your pouch. Those tickets and passports are the most important things you've got."

Other parents were saying the same kinds of things to their sons or daughters. Five kids from the youth group were going, along with sixteen adults. As the airline announced our boarding, the conversations changed to hugs and kisses.

"We'll miss you. You know that. But we know God's going with you," my dad said. "I just wish we could go too."

Mom started to cry. To Monica and me, the trip was like going off to camp. To Mom it was a whole different story. Only later did I realize that this was the first time my mom and I had ever *really* been separated. She had always been my main helper on things like camping trips. I didn't want to make a big deal out of this, and neither Monica nor I knew what to say.

We were glad when the flight attendant came up to us. "Let's get you boarded before the others. Can I have your tickets?"

Monica gave both our tickets to the flight attendant and followed her to the open door.

"Wait!" Pastor Rob called out. "Could we just wait for one minute more. We'd like to pray for everyone on the trip, including these two."

The flight attendant looked a little annoyed but finally agreed when she saw sixty or more people staring at her. "Okay, but please, just a minute."

"Gather around, folks." Our team formed a circle, and the families formed a circle around the outside of us. "Father, please be with these servants of Yours as we travel. Bring us back safely with good news from a distant land. In Jesus' name, amen."

The instant he said "amen," the flight attendant grabbed my wheelchair and headed me down the jetway. Monica quickly caught up with her. Pastor Rob had started a hymn whose words we could hear behind us: "Blest be the tie that binds . . ."

Once at the door of the plane, I transferred to a narrow little seat with wheels on it that could fit in the aisles of the plane. They folded up my wheelchair and took it down below to store in the baggage compartment.

"Please make sure it gets on, okay?" Monica said to the gate agent. "To my sister it's like her legs."

He nodded politely. "No problem. I'll take it down right now."

The flight attendant pulled me backwards down the aisle of the plane and stopped next to my seat. I transferred into the aisle seat and buckled in. Monica climbed over me into the middle seat. No one else was on the plane yet.

"So are you ready, sis?" she asked. "I mean, really ready?"

I understood her question. She wasn't asking about my toothbrushes or my passport that hung around my neck in a pouch. She was asking about my heart.

The question took my breath away—like when you go on a swing really fast and lose your stomach. We looked at each other with wide eyes.

"Too late now!" I laughed nervously.

Monica laughed too. We had gotten what we prayed for. There was no turning back.

✵ ✵ ✵

Our flight to Miami was full of fun. The airline had put all of us in one section, so it was like a big party. People traded seats often, talking to each other as if they hadn't seen each other in twenty years. Bags of cookies were passed back and forth. Some people were almost too rowdy; a pillow fight broke out.

We landed in Miami way behind schedule. We'd have to move quickly once everyone else got off the

plane to transfer to the next flight. The flight attendant warned us, "You'll have about ten minutes to get
from here to Gate 17. We hope that they won't have
boarded anyone else before you get there. Good luck."

Monica and I were ready, but my chair wasn't. It
was still down in the storage area of the plane.

"Where's the chair?" Monica asked the flight
attendant who was saying good-bye to people as they
got off the plane.

"They're working on it, kids. Just be patient. It's
probably stuck behind the baggage they're unloading
now."

"But we have to have it now to get to our flight,"
Monica pointed out. "You said we only had ten minutes
to get to the next gate."

"I know, but there's nothing I can do to get it off
sooner." The flight attendant looked at us with concern.
"Tell you what. Why don't you take this chair here to
the next gate, and we'll bring your chair there as soon
as we unload it." She pointed to an old, clunky chair
parked just outside the door of the plane. It was the
kind used to move people around the airport.

Monica and I looked at each other nervously. This
was our first test alone, as the rest of the group had
run on ahead of us. If we waited here for my chair, we

might miss the next plane. If we did as the flight attendant said, we'd probably make the plane, but we might arrive in Guatemala without my wheelchair.

"But what if the chair doesn't get loaded on the plane in time?" Monica asked.

"It will. Trust me," answered the flight attendant. "I'll keep a lookout for it myself and deliver it to your next plane. I promise. Now, please, you've got to hurry."

I transferred into the temporary chair, and Monica pushed me up the jetway toward the next gate where our plane would be waiting. Gate 17 was at the opposite end of the airport. It seemed miles away. "Hold on, Darcy. Here we go," Monica cried. We wove in and out of tourists and businessmen as if we were at the Indianapolis 500. Far ahead we could see the heads and backs of the others on our trip. One was on the lookout for us and turned around and waved. Monica ran all the faster to catch up.

"We'll make it, Darcy!" Monica shouted. "They're still loading people at the gate. I can see them."

My hands relaxed their grip on the chair as Monica slowed her pace. When we finally arrived at the gate, the attendant stopped the line of passengers getting on and waved us over. "Okay, you two, move quickly. Give me your tickets."

We obeyed and boarded the plane. "Can I sit by the window this time?" I asked Monica.

"Sure. We'll lift the middle arm of the chair, and you can slide across." She put our bags in the overhead compartment while I slid over. Once I was settled, my mind went back to my wheelchair.

"What if my wheelchair doesn't get on in time, Monica?" I looked at her with pleading eyes, as if she could—or should—do something.

"Let me see if I can get someone to check on it." She stood up to find a gate agent, but the aisles were jammed with people taking off their coats and loading things in the compartments above them. She looked in both directions but couldn't find anyone. The plane was quickly turning into a zoo.

"Darcy, the plane is packed, and they're all helping other passengers. Let's just pray about the chair, okay?" she said and sat down.

I bowed my head immediately and prayed, "Lord, please let my chair get on. You know I need it. I've got to have it with me!"

Monica added, "Please take control, Lord, over the baggage handlers. They already have to load 50 other wheelchairs going to Guatemala. Please be sure they add one more special one. In Jesus' name, amen."

I looked up at Monica again, still feeling helpless but at least knowing that God was in control and would work something out.

To take my mind off the chair, I stared at the window. I scanned the scene below me. There were tanker trucks, jeeps, workers wearing shorts, and a pilot checking tires. They seemed unconcerned with our mission and not the least bit worried about my problem. I felt like shouting out to them. But all I could do was pray and hope that God would answer soon.

Then as I watched the scene below me, I saw His answer in the distance. Piled on top of suitcases and boxes in a wagon was—my wheelchair!

"There it is, Monica!" I grabbed her arm. "It's over there!"

"Where?" she said, leaning over me and peering through the window.

"There!" I pointed.

She saw it immediately. "Yesss! Thank You, Lord!" God had been there for our first crisis.

Within several minutes our plane was completely loaded. It backed away from the gate and taxied toward the runway. The pilot made an announcement, the engine whined, and we rumbled down the runway at full speed. Then "lift off." This time we were *really* on our way.

As the plane banked, the flat south Florida landscape below me looked strangely beautiful. Everything glittered in the sun. White stucco houses looked like palaces, and swimming pools sparkled like diamonds. The ocean was a beautiful turquoise blue, and the empty everglades miles inland looked lush and green. Highways twisted in clean curves with cars, now looking like orderly matchbox toys, traveling on them. Tall office buildings stuck up high like upside down icicles, their windows reflecting the sun and the scene below.

By the time our plane climbed to 35,000 feet, I was exhausted. It had been a hectic day and one full of emotions. Others in our group also seemed tired. The rowdy atmosphere was gone. Shouts were replaced by whispers. You could tell that some were also getting nervous. I punched my pillow, closed my eyes, and joined several others who slept.

We traveled in sleepy silence for most of this flight. Only after we crossed the Gulf of Mexico and the pilot announced that our seatbelts should be fastened for landing did I look out the window again.

"Ladies and gentlemen, we will be making our approach to Guatemala soon and ask that you return to your seats so that we can begin our final descent. Please put your seats in the upright position . . ."

I looked out over the land below me. It was nothing like the garden-type scene I had viewed while leaving Miami. The emerald green of golf courses and pools was replaced by the dark green of a thick forest. The hills rolled on endlessly under their lush, dense covering of trees. Villages and towns spotted the landscape here and there but without the orderly connections of superhighways. There were fewer cars on the fewer roads, and most of the roads were dirt. What buildings I did see were low and reflected no light. In fact, there was no brightness at all. A haze covered everything. It made the green darker and more mysterious.

"So here we are," I said to Monica. "We're now entering the jungle zone." I made jungle-like noises, and we both laughed nervously.

The image I had in my mind of Guatemala shattered as soon as we taxied and parked at the gate. Though I had studied the country for social studies class (I had gotten an A on the project!) and thought I knew everything, I was shocked by what I saw as we got off the plane. The place was not at all like a jungle—hot and steamy. Instead it was cool and misty. Tall mountains towered behind us in the distance. It felt as if we had traveled north instead of south to get there.

"Quite a place, isn't it?" Mr. Wilcox said as we went to the terminal.

I nodded without saying anything. I was too busy looking around. Monica just stared too.

We all went through Immigration where they checked our passports and then through Customs where they checked our bags. They waved all of us through pretty quickly and didn't open anyone's suitcase. The 50 wheelchairs we had brought with us were put into containers for delivery after we arrived in the town.

Pastor Rob called our group together after the last person cleared Customs. "We're all going to get on this bus," he said. "Be sure you've got everything. From here we will be driving for about two hours. Please take any bathroom breaks before we leave in fifteen minutes."

We all looked at the bus to which he pointed. No one said it, but we all thought the same thing: *That bus is going to fit all of us in for a two-hour drive?*

The bus was old, short, and had balding tires. Long ago it had lost its original paint and was now dull beige with rust spots. Here and there someone had painted colorful designs, but even they were cracking and peeling. "It reminds me of a hippie bus I used to ride years ago," Mr. Wilcox laughed. The top of the bus was already loaded with old boxes. The engine was running, wheezing every now and then as if begging to be turned off to get a rest.

"Where do you think the wheelchair lift is located, Monica?" I asked with a straight face. Her first look of shock then gave way to a knowing smile. We burst out laughing.

The stress of everything strange, the long trip, the airport people speaking a steady stream of Spanish at 100 miles an hour all around us had overwhelmed us. My joke woke us out of our dream world. We realized things were going to be different. We would need a sense of humor if we were going to survive this trip.

Five

There was a good reason why our bus looked like it had been through a war.

It had!

Several years earlier civil war had broken out in the country. Guerrilla soldiers had used the bus to carry equipment secretly from across the border. A few bullet holes pierced the side.

Not only had guns taken a toll on the bus, but so had the road. The ride from the airport was the bumpiest, curviest, potholiest road I'd ever been on. The gears of the old bus ground as we bumpity-bumped our way over small rocks and large ruts. Several times we were thrown at least six inches into the air. Those standing in the aisle of the bus were constantly falling against the people sitting down, hitting them in the head with stuff they were holding. The bus was filled with laughter, whoops, and hollers as we held on to each other. We eyed the road ahead to see if we could predict the next bump.

Despite our group's circus mood, the driver didn't say a word or change his driving style. He just plowed ahead as if the road were fine and we were all a bunch of silly Americans. From time to time the bus stopped to pick up people walking along the road.

"Is this a public bus?" a man in front of me asked.

"Oh no, it belongs to the driver. He's just offering people a ride."

"Does he charge them money?"

"No, I don't think so."

The fun part of the ride grew old fast. The fumes from the bus, combined with the bumping and twisting, made my stomach feel awful. Keeping myself in my seat without leg muscles was hard, and I had to rely on Monica's tight hold on me, pressing me against the window and side of the bus.

"Are you okay?" she asked.

"Yeah, fine," I said, not really lying because even

though I wasn't feeling well, there was nothing I could do about it. I would stick it out, and I'd be fine.

I leaned my head against the window and looked at the scenery rolling by. It didn't change much. All I saw was green—trees and bushes packed tightly together, heavy with rain. The mist that hovered over the green carpet never seemed to move. It just hung there, the clouds and trees seeming to blend into one green-gray wall. I wondered if we would ever see the sun.

"Mr. Wilcox." I tapped on his shoulders. "Will the weather always be like this here?"

"Oh no. In another day or so it will all change. You'll see the sun every day, and there won't be any rain at all. It happens every July for two weeks."

That was good news because there was mud everywhere—thick and deep mud. I wondered how I would survive in my wheelchair if the town we were going to didn't have paved streets. I continued to look out the window. Every once in a while the mist would move, and I could see the top of a mountain, or I could peer down into a steep gully. Sometimes I could see a little mud and plaster house in the distance. I wondered what it would be like to be a kid living in a house like that, so far away from everything.

Things settled down in our bus after awhile. We

either got used to the bumps, or else the driver, sensing the problems they caused, actually tried to avoid them. Pastor Rob stood up at the front of the bus.

"Can I have your attention, folks?"

Those in the aisle turned around to face him. Conversations died down so that all we could hear was the engine, the sound of rain hitting the roof, and the slosh-sloshing of the windshield wipers.

"We're about half an hour away now, so I thought I'd give you some helpful information. This will make things run more smoothly when we get to the church.

"Each of you has been assigned to a family. You'll be staying with them the entire time. They're expecting you and are all looking forward to it. You'll be matched up with your host family when we arrive at the church. You'll take your bags off the bus and carry them into the church. Don't leave anything outside. We've been told that there are street kids who like to target visitors in order to steal their luggage and things. Once inside the church, line up along the front. We'll give a greeting to everyone, Pastor Zepeda will translate, and then we'll call out names to get you matched up. Any questions?"

"Yes," someone screamed from the back. "Where's

the nearest McDonalds?" Everyone laughed. Big Macs, Cokes, and fries seemed like something from another planet. Anyway I imagined that all our stomachs growled at the mention of food.

We eventually left the rolling, green mountainside and approached a small town, brown and gray with mud. Some streets were paved, but most of the roads were made of packed dirt or gravel and stone. Factories dotted the outskirts along with farm fields. There were a few cars on the road but not more than a dozen or so. The mist mixed with the rain in a depressing picture. I saw very few people outside.

When we finally pulled up at the church, I saw why we were there. It was badly in need of paint and repair. It looked worse than what I had seen on the slides. The building was small, too small for a church, I thought. The roof was made of tin sheets—some gray, some rusting. There were two small windows in front with a potted plant in each.

We got off the bus nervously and made our way into the church without much trouble. All did as they were told, unlike the kids on some school field trips I had been on. Most were nervous about meeting their host families, especially those who knew no Spanish at all. I was glad Monica and I knew a little from school and that we had practiced. At least we'd be able to know what we were eating and where the bathrooms were.

Although the church building was run-down and small, there was something special about it. Only a few windows let in a little gray light, and yet the room somehow felt bright and warm. Guatemalans in brightly colored clothing filled the pews.

We lined up along the front of the church. I wheeled to the far right side and scanned the scene. There were close to 100 people in the room. I stared at each one of them in turn. The faces of the people were dark, their hair a deep black. I was struck with the kindness in their eyes and their smiles.

Oh, the smiles!

After a few moments I realized I wasn't the only one staring. The Guatemalans were staring at me! Kids especially pointed in my direction and whispered among themselves.

"Feeling like you're on display?" Monica leaned over and asked.

"Yeah," I said. "It's like they've never seen a wheelchair before. Especially a twelve-year-old American girl in a wheelchair." I wondered if I might have been the first.

Pastor Rob stepped forward from the line with Pastor Zepeda.

"Greetings from your brothers and sisters in Christ from the U.S.," he said. "We're glad to be here after a long trip."

Pastor Zepeda translated into Spanish.

"We live far away from you. But because we all love our Lord Jesus Christ, we feel very close to you. And we look forward to our two weeks of working with you."

The audience clapped after the translation.

"And now we're going to match you with your families," Pastor Zepeda said as he turned to face our group.

I looked out over the sea of faces, wondering who our family would be.

Pastor Rob called out the American names while Pastor Zepeda called out the Guatemalans. Each stepped forward and greeted one another in the center aisle and then left the room together.

After five or six names, Monica and I were called. A man and his wife stood up immediately when Pastor Zepeda called their name—Mr. and Mrs. Gonzalez. Three children followed them down the aisle. As we approached the center together, I saw the faces of our hosts change. Though they were still smiling, question marks seem to cover their faces. I wondered if they hadn't been told about my disability.

"How . . . are . . . you?" the father asked slowly in English.

"Fine. I mean *bien*," Monica replied.

"*Bien*," I repeated, mumbling my first Spanish word. I don't think anyone heard it.

We shook hands awkwardly. The three kids hid behind their mom and peeked. I tried to smile and catch their attention, but they pulled back behind the parents even more.

The father pointed down the aisle and motioned for us to go.

"*Gracias*," I said, thanking him. I expected him to smile at my second Spanish word. He seemed not to notice that I had just spoken Spanish. *Whew, this won't be easy!*

We were led outside to the street where we headed to the right. The rain had slowed to a light drizzle. Our host carried the bags. His girls ran on ahead while their mother walked close by Monica and me.

"How's the ride?" Monica asked me.

"Okay, so far. A little bumpier than I expected, but I'm okay." I held on to the small bag on my lap as

Monica pushed me. We passed by small apartment buildings, stores, and what must have been a gas station— a building with two old cars, a red gas pump, and a mechanic working under the hood of a car.

The kids arrived at the house ahead of us. Two ran in, and one lingered outside waiting for us. The father then entered with our bags. We followed. There was just a small step to get into the house, but once in, I could see that there'd be no problem getting around in my wheelchair.

"Come," the father said. He led us down a hallway to our room. It had two beds, a dresser, and a window. Next to our room was a bathroom.

"Looks like I'll be crawling on the floor to get into the bathroom," I whispered to Monica as I looked at the width of the doorway to the bathroom. I would never fit the wheelchair in, but I could get on the floor and, with Monica's help, get to the toilet.

"Hey, cheer up," Monica said. "This'll be just like camping."

"You're the one that will need cheering up," I said. "You'll be doing all the lifting!"

Our tour of the house completed, we were led back to the main living area. The area had a kitchen on one side, a table in the middle, and some chairs at the far side. One lamp hung from the ceiling. A book-shelf topped with knickknacks and a photo leaned against a wall. And that's all there was. It was unlike any living room I had ever seen.

The table had been laid out with plates and cups ahead of time. We could smell the cooking and knew that Mrs. Gonzalez had prepared quite a bit ahead of time for us. We were told by Mr. Wilcox that our host families would probably treat us royally and that there would be a special meal when we arrived.

"Eat," Mrs. Gonzalez said in English, directing us to the table. We would eventually learn that it was her favorite command and the only English she knew!

Mr. Gonzalez called to the kids who had followed us all around the house, spying on everything we did or said.

"What's your name?" Monica asked the oldest girl in Spanish.

"Fabiana," she whispered.

The middle girl answered, "Margarita," upon hearing her oldest sister tell her name.

The youngest blurted out, "Antonia."

Mr. Gonzalez smiled proudly as if his girls were prized jewels. The oldest looked about eight or nine, the youngest maybe four.

Mrs. Gonzalez brought the food to the table after we were all seated. There were platefuls of black beans and fried bananas. There was grilled meat mixed with tomatoes and onions too. Mrs. Gonzalez seemed pleased with what was on the table. I could tell she had worked hard at it. If my mom back home had served the same meal, I probably would have complained about something or other being too this or too that. But I was hungry, and just being there helped me to get over whatever hang-ups I had about food. It was a part of the adventure, and so I accepted, even enjoyed, the meal.

Monica and I fumbled through the meal with our Spanish. We were able to tell them about our home by pointing to our state on a map of the United States. Monica did most of the talking. I understood her Spanish a little but couldn't understand theirs because they spoke so quickly.

After supper Mr. Gonzalez got up and went to the bookcase. He brought back a Spanish Bible. The kids, squirming up till now, suddenly got quiet.

"I read," he said. "Sorry, Spanish. You understand." He smiled.

He read the Bible for perhaps a minute or two and then closed it gently. His hands smoothed out the cover, and he stared at it as if it were his finest treasure.

"Pray," he said.

We all bowed our heads as he prayed. I still didn't understand a word he said, but I knew it was something special. I got chills up and down my spine, and then a warm feeling oozed all over me. I could almost feel it in my legs. I was listening to a man talk to God in a language I didn't understand, and yet I knew that he loved God. In the middle of a poor house with no TV, VCR, radio, carpeting, couches, stereos, or phones, this man was happy, and his kids were happy. God lived there, it seemed, and I felt special to be there with them.

❖ ❖ ❖

Monica and I lay in bed that night and talked like we had never talked before. We recounted the day with laugher and with awe.

"And did you see that oven? Mom would have flipped. I don't know how Mrs. Gonzalez can cook with that thing!"

"Yeah. I was scared of eating, but that stuff was actually good. I could have eaten it all myself."

"You almost did. You reminded me of Josh. I just hope you don't have stomach problems. I don't want to have to cart you back and forth to the bathroom all night!"

I shuddered in the darkness, picturing that bathroom again.

"You know what I noticed most?" I asked.

"What?"

"The time after supper."

"Yeah. That was something, wasn't it?"

"What was neat to me was that I didn't feel rushed to go anywhere. And I wasn't bored. I wish we could do that at home."

"We could, Darcy, if we'd only give Dad a chance, but we're so busy trying to get out of Bible reading time that we don't stop to enjoy it. Why do you think it means more here?"

"Maybe it's because that's all there is here. No TV. No cheerleading practices. No malls where you can hang out with your friends. You get a chance to be still and listen."

We lay quietly in the dark after a while. The thought of doing without things and events made me wonder, *Why do I have that stuff anyway? And why do we always seem to be so busy?* I couldn't remember any supper where we weren't in a hurry to go somewhere. And Mom had to drive us places all the time.

She was always kidding about having to be our taxi driver.

Even with all the excitement of the day, sleep came quickly. I don't remember when I drifted off. I only remember that the rain had picked up again, and it lulled me to sleep.

Six

I could hardly believe my eyes the next morning. Was I still in Guatemala? Rather than the dark, gray blanket that had covered the sky and everything around me the day before, bright sunshine was everywhere. Our room was filled with it. Even the shadows on the wall seemed bright.

I quickly rolled out of bed and into my wheelchair to look outside. I saw a different world through the iron grating that covered the window. Houses were no longer one long row of brown, but rather separate homes of pinks and tans. Women walked the street in their Indian clothing, looking festive and alive. It was like watching a Disney parade.

"Monica, come look! The sun's out," I said. Monica stirred under her covers, slowly coming to life. She never was a morning person.

"What time is it?"

"Uh, eight o'clock, I think. We're in the same time zone as back home."

"Did you say eight?"

"Yeah."

"Darcy, hurry! We've got to be at the church by nine!" Monica jumped out of bed, her eyes still half-closed.

"What's the rush?" I asked. "We've got an hour."

"I know but I have to get a shower, get dressed, do my hair . . ."

I looked at her mussed-up hair and the panicked look on her face. I had to laugh. "Monica, get real! This is not a European vacation. Who cares what you look like? You don't need to impress any of the boys. Just throw on jeans and a T-shirt and you'll be ready. C'mon, help me to the bathroom."

Monica smiled and realized I was right. Spending hours each day getting ready was another of those American teenage habits we were going to have to forget. It felt strange at first, but after awhile we got used to it and in time were glad for it. Mom would later wonder whether or not we had become too relaxed about it.

We ate a small breakfast of scrambled eggs and beans and then left for the church. Mr. Gonzalez and Fabiana escorted us. I was glad they did. Although it wasn't far, we would have lost our way. Landmarks didn't look familiar, and there were no signs along the way. We arrived at the church in about ten minutes.

"Well, Darcy and Monica, how are you this morning?" Mrs. Wilcox greeted us. "How did you two sleep?"

"Fine. I slept the whole night through," I answered.

"And your family? Do you enjoy them? Can you talk with one another?"

"Yeah, kinda," Monica said, looking at Mr. Gonzalez. He smiled as he and Fabiana turned and headed back home.

"They talk so fast," I whispered in case Mr. Gonzalez understood me. "I can't keep up."

"I know what you mean. Our family is the same way," Mr. Wilcox agreed.

We filed into the church together with others who had been brought by their host families and sat in the pews. Pastor Rob got up to speak after everyone arrived.

"Well, here we are, folks. It's a beautiful day, isn't it? We're fortunate the rain stopped in time for our work. Before we pray and get the day started, let's go over the work assignments for the day. Now remember, we've got three teams. Team 1, you'll start on your construction projects here. There are two Sunday school rooms that need to be built out back. The outside needs painting also, and so you can get two or three of your members to start on that.

"Team 2, you'll need to do the survey in the town to find out who needs a wheelchair. Pastor Zepeda has given me a list, but we have more wheelchairs than he thought we would, so we'll help him do the survey to add to his list. Darcy, I would have had you go with this team, but I think we'll save you for later. You can join Team 3, which will be doing drama and music in the town square. Orlando here, one of the young people from the church who speaks excellent English, will take your team and show you around. He'll help you set up the puppet show and will also interpret for you. You're also fortunate to have Rick Rios as your leader. Rick is a college student majoring in Bible. He speaks terrific Spanish and has plans to go to the mission field."

The entire group was excited about their jobs, with the new sunny day and the prospect of helping people. My job on Team 3 was to operate one of the puppets. Some of us in the youth group also put together a singing group that could sing choruses as a part of the outreach.

"Okay, everyone, we're going to get started. Let's pray before you all go your separate ways," Pastor Rob said after reviewing details for another ten minutes. "Lord, we're Your servants today. Use us according to Your plan. May people sense Your love for them and want to know more about why we're here and what You've done for them on the cross."

Amen, I said in my heart. *You know I'm ready, Lord. Use me today in a big way.*

"Okay, listen up," Rick announced to our group after the others split up and went to their areas. "Our goal today is to attract as much attention as we can to the church and to the outreach events. We're going to be inviting people to come out to church on Sunday for a special meeting. We'll also hand out these tracts." He held up a full-color tract printed in Spanish. "If you have the opportunity to talk to someone about Jesus, go ahead. Don't be shy. Some of our Guatemalan friends will be joining us and can do the job for you if you can't speak the language. Orlando and I will also be around if you need any help. Any questions?" We were all silent, just waiting to be told what to do. "Okay. Here are your parts for the puppet show. Let's take the puppet equipment with us and move out!"

We excitedly responded with "Yah's" and "Whoof-whoof's" as if we were a football team.

The center of town where we set up our show was nothing fancy. There was a park that wasn't much of a park— just a large area with concrete tiles surrounded by bushes. It was more like a courtyard.

Within minutes of setting up the stage, we had a curious crowd. Most of them were kids, but a few adults had gathered too. When we told the group what we'd be doing, a number of kids ran to get their friends.

The kids who remained did more than watch. They squeezed in close around us, trying to touch and play with the puppets. Orlando and Rick had to be strict with them. After all, it would have spoiled it for the kids to see the puppets before they came to life. Some of the kids hung around me, speaking in Spanish and pointing to my wheelchair with great interest.

"*Silla de ruedas*," I said in Spanish. "This is my wheelchair."

They nodded. *Oh good, they understand!* "I'm Darcy."

Some laughed at the sound of my name. Others called out their names. We talked mostly about objects right around us to keep the conversation simple. Monica pitched in with her Spanish, and that helped a lot. We smiled after we gave each object its Spanish and English names—shoes, shirt, hair, nose, etc.

"Darcy, you really need to get in your place over here," Rick called out after a while. "The stage is set up, and you need to go in first, in the middle." I moved quickly and took my place.

"Please leave now," Rick said in Spanish to the kids that had followed me behind the stage. They obeyed and took their places in front of the stage, eager for the show to start.

All but one of the kids moved—that is. He was a lost-looking boy, staring at me up and down and touching my wheelchair. He didn't say a word, and he didn't smile. His dark eyes were surrounded by a dirty face that looked like it had not been washed in a year. He was rather skinny and short. His body looked about seven or eight years old, but his face was somehow much older.

"Move," I heard Orlando say to the boy in Spanish. The boy didn't move.

"Go away," Orlando said again, walking closer to the boy and me.

The boy still did not move. Orlando had to grab the boy by the arm and lead him to join the rest of the kids. When Orlando returned to us, he explained, "That's Luis. He's one of the town trouble-makers. He doesn't have a mom or dad, and he hangs out with the street gangs. Some say he's loco—crazy. Others say he's cursed. He lives on the street somewhere and is always a pest. No one wants him. He steals a lot and always causes trouble. Watch out for him. You'll see."

I couldn't imagine Luis being a trouble-maker, but I saw soon enough. We were halfway through our puppet show when Luis got up and began walking around. He pushed some kids over. He then walked all the way up front and began reaching for the puppets. I panicked when he grabbed for mine. I didn't know what to do.

"Luis!" Orlando and others called out. "Sit down!"

The boy ignored them and tried to reach over the front of the puppet stage, but we had all pulled back our puppets. Seeing that he couldn't get a puppet from there, he came around the corner of the stage and would nearly have taken over one of our jobs had we not been firm. I was afraid. Luis did indeed seem crazy. It was as if he didn't know anything about manners or was in another world.

Orlando and Rick managed to take Luis off to the side and to the other end of the courtyard so we could finish our puppet show. Despite the rough start, the people like it. We were doing the story of Jonah. One of the church members narrated the story as we acted it out. Everyone clapped and cheered when we were done. The musicians took over next, singing English as well as Spanish songs. Our young singing group sang choruses and taught one of them to the kids.

When our program was finished, we walked into the crowd and handed out fliers and tracts. The kids took them eagerly. The adults were not as excited, but they were polite. Some said they'd like to read it. Others said they already went to church.

"Time for lunch," Monica announced as we finished handing out the fliers. "Rick's waving us over to head in his direction. We're supposed to go back to church, I think."

"Sure," I answered, surprised that the morning had gone so fast. There was still a crowd of kids around me, touching my wheelchair and talking a mile a minute. "Let me tell these kids we're leaving, Monica."

"I go," I said, turning to the kids as I made a hand motion. They seemed to understand and made their way in the opposite direction.

All but Luis again. He had sneaked back to the crowd after the show and had stood right behind me while I handed out tracts and fliers. I could tell he was there because he smelled like he had never taken a bath in his life. I wheeled around quickly and faced him head-on. I was going to teach this kid a thing or two about manners! If six other kids had understood my Spanish and left me, surely this kid could too.

"Go away!" I said again. I thrust my hand and finger out as if chasing away a dog. "Now!"

Luis didn't move. He just smiled at me. I was beginning to get angry at him, but something made me stop. His head cocked from one side to another. He then looked in the direction to which I pointed. His smile finally left his face, and he turned to go, realizing I was not happy with him. His shoulders slumped as he headed toward a row of old houses. My heart ached for him, and I felt bad that I had treated him that way.

"Luis!" I called out. "Wait, Luis." He didn't turn back. "Luis!"

Luis moved on without a reply or so much as a glance.

Puzzled and feeling even worse, I wheeled in his direction. I repeated his name over and over again as I got closer and closer. Luis finally did turn around but only after I tugged on his shirt. He looked sad and hurt.

"*Comprende*, Luis? Do you understand?" I asked in Spanish. He stared at me without emotion. "Luis, *comprende*?" I said in a louder voice. "Do you understand?"

I was sure I was saying it correctly in Spanish. That was one of the first words I had learned.

"Lord, how do I let him know I'm sorry?"

Luis just stared at me blankly.

"Luis, can you hear my voice?" He stared at me. I pointed to my ears. "Can you hear?" No response. I looked back at the park area and spotted Rick about to leave for church. "Rick, come here," I called out.

Rick left the group he was with and joined Luis and me.

"Can you ask Luis if he can hear me?"

Rick was puzzled but translated as I asked.

Luis looked up at Rick with a blank stare.

"Maybe he doesn't speak Spanish," Rick said. "Remember, some people in Guatemala only speak native Indian. Let me try a few words I know."

Rick tried, but there was still no response from Luis.

"I'm stumped, Darcy. There's no other language he would know if he's from around here. Sorry, I can't help you. But remember, this kid is trouble. He could be putting on a strange act just to get attention. We've got to get back, Darcy. C'mon," Rick said as he headed in the direction of the church.

Luis and I were left standing together. His eyes still looked deep into mine, as if doubting my intentions.

"Luis, we've got to find out if you can hear." I pointed to my ears and spoke in English. "Can you hear?" Luis finally touched his ear. It wasn't much of a response, but at least it was a start.

My mind raced to come up with an answer. "I know," I said out loud. I closed my eyes for couple of seconds and then touched Luis's eyes and asked him to close them. He understood my command. I wanted his eyes to be closed while I did my experiment.

After he closed his eyes, I reached up next to his ear and snapped my finger. No response. Next I clapped loudly as close to his ears as possible. He didn't flinch at all. Then I shouted his name as loudly as I could, directly in his ear.

His eyes stayed shut. He didn't move a muscle.

"I bet you're deaf," I said aloud. I reached up to his eyes and touched the closed eyelids. He opened his eyes and looked at me curiously.

"Yes, Luis, I think you're deaf!"

Seven

I explained my theory about Luis to Monica and the Gonzalez family that night while we ate supper. I had convinced Orlando to come to the house to translate for me. "Deaf," I said to Orlando, pointing to my ears. "Tell them Luis is deaf."

A look of happy surprise came over Mr. Gonzalez's face as Orlando translated. "Yes, yes, that explains it," our host replied. "He doesn't hear. He's bad because he doesn't hear!" he said in Spanish. Orlando translated for us.

"That's part of it," I answered, glad that someone accepted my idea. "It's not just that he doesn't hear. It's that no one's taken the time to teach him. That's what

---

I think." I rattled on at eighty miles per hour about what it must be like for Luis, why he did what he did to get attention, and what should be done to help him. Orlando translated for me, though I don't think he was convinced. That didn't stop Orlando from telling me about Luis.

"Doesn't he have any family—no mother or father?" I asked.

"No," Orlando answered. "He lives on the street. He doesn't have any family. He begs and steals to get by."

"But couldn't someone take care of him?"

"There isn't enough to go around, Darcy. Families are having a hard enough time making a living without worrying about all these homeless kids. And quite frankly these street kids can be pretty tough. People don't want anything to do with them."

We ended our time around the table in prayer. Orlando excused himself and left for home. Monica and I were both very tired after our first day and headed for bed.

I lay awake in bed that night, thinking about Luis. I couldn't imagine growing up on my own without a family and without anyone in the town caring about me or even liking me. My heart went out to Luis. I thought about him late into the night. My last picture of him in my mind's eye was of him walking away from me, his shoulders slumped, his eyes sad.

I woke up the next morning with a start, Luis still on my mind. "Monica, c'mon, let's go. We've got some work to do."

"Go where?"

"Into the town. To find Luis."

"And what are we going to do?" she yawned her sarcastic question.

"I don't know, but we'll find out when we see him."

We left right after breakfast, giving us plenty of time to show up at church. I really had no plan in mind. A part of me wanted to solve all the boy's problems and make him hear again. I didn't know what to do, but I thought that we had to start somewhere.

It didn't take long to find Luis. Our white skin was like a magnet, and soon we were surrounded by kids.

"Luis," we asked the kids. "Where's Luis?"

Two or three kids took off down an alley and reappeared with him in tow. His face beamed when he saw us. He ran to meet me.

"Good morning, Luis," I said. The kids stood

around us—some giggling, others gaping jealously at the attention he was getting.

"Do you want to go for a walk?" I asked. I put my hand out and made my two fingers pretend that they were walking on the hand. I pointed to the three of us—Monica, Luis, and me.

He looked at me, puzzled. Monica gave it a shot. She marched in place for a moment, then pointed to Luis and me, and then pointed in different directions.

It was like a light bulb switching on in Luis's head. He nodded with a broad smile. Then he reached out for my hand and pulled me.

"No. Wait!" I yelled. "I'll fall."

Monica grabbed Luis and shook her head no. "Push," she said and then got behind me and showed him how. He understood instantly and stepped into Monica's place. We were off on our adventure with a dozen kids following us!

Luis gave us a long, depressing tour. We had seen a nice part of the town on our first day. But Luis showed us the way many other people lived. Small shacks made of scrap lumber and tin lined the dirt streets. It was hard to imagine anyone living in such a place, but I saw people everywhere. A garbage dump nearby smelled terrible. Several people were picking through the dump. An old man was squatting in the middle of it, eating what was left from someone's meal. Ugh!

After I thought I had seen the worst, Luis took us to what we thought was just another pile of junk. Over and over again he pointed to himself and then to the junk. It took us a long time to figure out that the "junk" was his home!

He smiled as he showed us his bed, his extra set of clothes, and a ball. And that was all he owned. Monica and I looked at each other in shock, and I started to cry.

Luis lost his smile. He shook his head back and forth as if to say I shouldn't feel sorry for him. He pointed to himself, then to his bed, and then to himself and smiled again.

"Monica, we've got to do something."

"But what? He's got no parents. No one likes him, and you have to admit, Darcy, he is trouble, if you know what I mean. Besides, he can't hear or talk. What could we do?"

My mind raced for a moment, searching for an idea. Even if we gave him money, I knew it wouldn't last. It seemed hopeless until I remembered something a missionary had said at our church once: "Give a man a fish, and he'll eat for a day. Teach him to fish, and he'll eat for life."

"That's it!" I said out loud. "That's what we'll do. We'll teach him!"

"Teach him what? What are you talking about?"

"We'll teach him to talk."

"Darcy, get real. The kid can't talk at all—not Spanish and definitely not English." Monica rolled her eyes.

"I know that. But we can still teach him to, you know, communicate. We'll teach him sign language."

"But we don't know sign language."

"That's okay. We'll just teach him something that makes sense to us. C'mon. It'll be fun. Like the story of Helen Keller."

Monica usually avoided getting into my schemes, but this time she had no choice. Wherever I went, she had to go too. She saw that I wasn't going to back down and leave Luis.

"All right. But this is kinda silly, don't you think?"

"Why?"

"Well, we came down here to help out the church, to tell people about Jesus. Don't you remember you were going to give speeches about your life and stuff?"

I would have come up with some kind of argument, but Luis didn't give me a chance. He had gotten bored with our conversation and had wandered off.

"Wait!" I called out and caught up with him. I held his arm gently and spoke to Monica. "You're right, Monica. We did come here for something else. But Luis is here for a reason too. I just can't ignore him. Besides, there'll be time for the other stuff, I'm sure."

I didn't mean to sound like the boss, but I was so sure that this was how we should spend our time that Monica backed down. "Just call me your servant," she said sarcastically but with a nice smile.

"Come with us," she motioned to Luis. He obeyed, and we headed for the church. We went in silence, once again passing the row of shacks and moving into the main section of town. The work crew had already started working on the new rooms and the painting when we arrived. The three of us stopped just outside and sat on the edge of the street.

"Okay, Lesson One," I said. "What do we teach him?"

"Let's see if he really is an orphan."

I pointed to a small girl across the street and then to her mother. Next I pointed at Luis and then up high, while shrugging my shoulders as if to ask a question. I did it again, this time adding motions for long hair and hugging. Luis stared at me and then shook his head. It took several tries, but it finally worked. He caught on and shook his head no without emotion.

Luis got the idea that we really wanted to talk to him and get to know him. He started pacing up and down excitedly like a lion in a cage. He caught on so well that he finally asked us a question before we could think of another one for him.

He pointed to my wheelchair. Then he pointed for me to get out and walk.

I shook my head no.

"How are you going to explain this one?" Monica asked.

I shrugged my shoulders but gave it a shot. I started by pointing to a car across the street. With one hand I motioned as if it were coming down the street, while with my other hand I made a running motion. Then I made my two hands bump together. I flopped to one side of my chair as if unconscious. Then I "woke up," pointed to my legs, and shook my head no. "They won't move," I said in English.

"Agh!" Luis grunted out loud, obviously upset by my story. It was his first sound.

"It's okay," I told him, holding his arm. "I can't walk, but you can't hear. We both are different."

I pointed to his ears. I clapped my hands and then shook my head and pointed to him. Having not heard a sound before, I wondered if he even knew that my hands made a sound that he couldn't hear.

He shook his head.

So he did know he couldn't hear. Our lessons in sign language were getting us someplace.

"I wonder if he's ever been to church," Monica said. She pointed to the church behind us and then to him. "Have you been inside?" she motioned.

Luis didn't seem to understand.

"Let's just take him inside," I said.

Monica took his hand and led him to the entrance. Pastor Rob was nailing up the door frame for the painters.

"Hi, Pastor Rob," I said. "Can we go inside? I mean, they're not working in there, are they?"

"No. Go on in. Let me just move this stepladder here and get out of your way. Who's your friend?" he asked as he made way for us.

"This is Luis. He's a deaf boy who lives on the street."

Pastor Rob reached out his hand to Luis with a big smile. "Hello, young fellow. Nice to meet you."

Luis pulled back, unsure of the big, smiling American man.

"It's okay, Luis. He won't hurt you. He's my pastor." We didn't try to explain in signs to Luis. I just went on ahead into the sanctuary. "We wanted Luis to see what a church is like, Pastor Rob."

"Sure. You'll be surprised, by the way, at all the work they've done on the classrooms."

We entered the room. There was no one else inside, but we could hear the sound of hammers and saws on the other side of the building. There were also some workers on the roof, nailing something.

Luis looked around. We weren't sure what he was thinking. He went to the left wall and touched it, then glided his hand along the wall as he walked forward to the front. He was lost in thought as he reached the platform, climbed a couple of steps, and moved to the far wall. He stopped suddenly when he came to the cross hanging in the center. He stepped back to examine the scene. We moved closer.

"He doesn't know anything about it, I bet," Monica whispered.

"Monica, you don't have to whisper," I answered. "Anyway how could Luis possibly understand. I doubt that anyone ever tried to explain it. I mean, it would be pretty hard."

Monica and I looked at each other at the same time.

"Are you thinking what I'm thinking?" I asked.

"Yes, but how? How could we possibly explain it?"

"Pictures," I said.

"Of God?"

"No. I mean yes. Kind of. My Bible has pictures in the back. We could show him the pictures of Adam and Eve and then show Jesus and the cross."

"We can show the pictures, all right, but they won't mean anything to him."

"Probably, Monica, but we've got to try. Let's just see what happens, okay?" I asked.

Monica went up on the platform and tapped Luis on the shoulder. He jumped in fright and pointed to the cross.

"Come over here with us." Monica motioned. "We want to tell you what it's about." She brought him to the front pew, sat him down between the two of us, and then got his attention. "Luis. That's a cross. Jesus died there. We're going to tell you why."

I took out my Bible and opened to the pictures in the back. We went page by page, explaining about

Adam and Eve doing a bad thing and about Moses taking his people to Israel. We showed him the picture of Jesus as a baby, then of Him teaching and helping people. Then we turned to the picture of Jesus on the cross, dying for our sins.

We did our best to sign ideas to him and point to the different parts of the pictures, but it was obvious that Luis was lost. We hadn't been able to explain anything.

"This isn't working, Darcy," Monica finally said.

"I know. But let's just pray. This is one of those impossible things we should have prayed about before."

We bowed our heads and began to pray. Strangely enough, Luis didn't move from his seat. Usually when Monica and I had a long conversation, Luis would get bored and wander off.

It was while we were praying that an idea came to me. I had opened my eyes to see what Luis was doing. As I did so, I looked at my hands. There on my right wrist was a friendship bracelet with colored beads in the colors of the wordless Bible. The wordless Bible was made up of five colors, each standing for a different part of how we can be saved and know Jesus.

I held on to Luis's arm as Monica said, "Amen."

"Luis, look at me," I said. I got his attention and

pointed to the bracelet I had taken off. I pointed to the black bead and then to my heart. "Bad!" I said and made a sad face. I pointed to Luis's heart and repeated "Bad!" with a sad face. Then I pointed to Adam and Eve and did the same thing.

Luis seemed to catch on. He pointed to his heart and nodded. He slapped his hands and made an angry face.

Encouraged, I pointed to the red bead and then to the picture of Jesus on the cross. I showed Luis the blood in the picture and then pointed back to the red bead. "Jesus died on the cross for my bad heart," I explained.

Luis's face seemed sadder.

"But," I held on to Luis, "my heart is now good. Look, the white bead!" I pointed to the white bead and then to my heart. "Luis, Christ dying on the cross made my black heart white." I did this with motions and the beads, this time pointing to Luis's heart.

"Good Darcy," I said. "And good Luis, if you believe that Jesus died for you, and you are sorry."

I realized what I was trying to say was getting a little difficult. "Keep praying while I do this," I urged Monica.

"You got it, kid. You're doing great."

I pointed to the green bead. "Because of Jesus you and I can have joy and grow every day." I pointed to Jesus' disciples in the Bible. I pointed at the church around us. "You, Luis. You come to church and make friends with people here. People here love you." I pointed to Monica. "Monica loves you." I made the sign for love, my arms hugging myself. "Jesus loves you," I signed.

Luis, for some unexplained reason, took hold of my hand and smiled. Then he did the most amazing thing. He repeated everything back to me. He pointed to his heart and frowned. Then he pointed to Jesus in the Bible and to the cross and to the red bead. Then he smiled and pointed to his heart and to the white bead. He pointed to the green bead and to Monica and me and to the church building. Then he smiled and hugged himself.

His face changed though. He suddenly grasped at the air and pulled his arms to his heart with a look of wanting something.

"Do you think he understands, Darcy? He seems to be asking for something."

I looked deeply into Luis's eyes. "Yes. I think he wants Jesus in his heart," I said.

"What if we prayed with him?" Monica said. "We

could pray for him, and I think God would hear his prayer through us."

I folded Luis's hands to pray. "This is how we do it," I said. "We're going to pray."

"Dear Lord," I said, "Luis really knows he needs You. He hasn't been able to read or to hear about You, but You know what his heart is like. He's shown us that he knows he's bad and that he wants You. That's what You want from people, isn't it? So please come into his heart, Lord, and make him a new person. Only You can do that because he can't talk to You right now."

I looked up from my prayer and reached out for Luis's hands. He opened his eyes at my touch. I smiled and nodded my head and then signed, "Jesus is in your heart. He loves you. You're not bad."

The three of us sat and stared at each other. Luis had the biggest smile on his face. Something had changed in his life.

"Way to go, Luis," I finally said. "You're a Christian now."

Eight

Luis sat on the floor with a large smile on his face, looking back and forth at Monica and me.

"Are you sure he wasn't, you know, just copying us?" I could tell Monica hated to ask the question. We had no way of really knowing, but it seemed to me that somehow Luis did understand that he was a sinner and that he had invited Jesus into his heart.

"Let's just trust God, okay, Monica?" I answered. "And let's go tell the others."

"Follow us, Luis." Monica motioned. "Let's go tell Pastor Rob."

We turned around and headed toward the back of the church. Pastor Rob had just finished painting the doorway and was rinsing out his brush in a bucket.

"Pastor Rob!" I called out. "You gotta hear this. Luis just became a Christian!"

Pastor Rob looked up while still squeezing the ends of the brush. "Oh?" he asked slowly. "And how do you know that?"

"Because we helped him."

"Yes, really," Monica added. "We shared the story about Jesus, using pictures and also Darcy's friendship bracelet. You know, the wordless Bible."

Pastor Rob smiled, but he looked like he wasn't convinced. He studied Luis, as if looking for something.

Orlando, who had been painting the window trim next to Pastor Rob, wasn't as kind. "It would be nice, Darcy, but I doubt he really did. The boy doesn't understand. He's just a street boy who wants to be liked by the Americans. He wants something from you. He'll nod his head and agree to anything you want him to."

"But he did accept Jesus!" I insisted. "I'll show you," I nearly yelled, which brought other workers to where the five of us were standing. I felt as if Luis and I were suddenly on trial. Monica, Luis, and I all felt it and huddled close to each other.

"Luis." Monica touched his hand. "Let's show them." She pointed to her heart and to Luis's heart. He frowned and slapped his hand to show "bad." Monica began the next step, but Luis figured out what she was doing and went on with the rest of the story. He made a cross in the air and then brought it to his chest. He smiled. Then he pointed to everyone and made the sign for love.

There were encouraging smiles from a few, but it seemed most of the people still doubted. I had to admit that any two-year-old or even a monkey might have been able to imitate what we had taught him. But then Luis did something that made the hairs on my neck stand up in a good way.

He looked around the group, sensing the doubts. So he pointed to himself and then looked up, motioning with his finger at the same time to the sky.

"Heaven!" I shouted. "He's going to heaven!"

Monica and I looked at each other in disbelief and then at Luis. Monica hugged him.

"What are you so excited about?" Orlando asked. "It still doesn't mean he understands. He's just copying you."

"But that's the point," I explained. "We taught him all those things he showed you, but we forgot to do the last bead on my friendship bracelet—the gold one. We forgot to tell him about heaven! Don't you see? He learned that on his own! God taught him that!"

Pastor Rob stepped in at this point. "Darcy and Monica, what you're telling us is really important. Are you absolutely sure you didn't tell him about heaven?"

"Absolutely. And besides we wouldn't know how to begin to describe heaven," Monica answered.

Pastor Rob turned to everyone there. "Folks, it says in the Bible that God speaks to our spirit and that sometimes things in this world that people consider foolish are actually wise and can understand the things of God. I think we all ought to pray for Luis and trust God regarding what happened. I know it's hard to believe, but Darcy and Monica might be right. Time will tell, don't you think?"

It was not the kind of support I was looking for from Pastor Rob. I really wanted him to say that he absolutely believed Luis was a Christian. But I realized it was the best he could do at the moment. There were too many people there who looked as if they had doubts, including Orlando and several other Guatemalans. Perhaps they knew Luis too well.

❦

* * *

Luis and I spent the rest of the day together. I tried to teach him as much as I could. We awkwardly made up sign language for *church, boy, girl, paint, tree*. It soon got to be a game. We laughed at our attempts to first come up with a hand sign and then to try and remember three minutes later what we had decided.

"I've got to write these down, Luis," I said, stopping at one point to get a notebook out of my bag. I wrote down the word and then a short description of how to make the sign. It was hard work, and I nearly gave up when I thought of Luis. *He'll never learn to read, I bet—let alone learn English.*

Our "talks" continued late into the afternoon. Luis was much calmer than before. He had always been jumpy and nervous, running back and forth or touching things. Now he walked with his hands in his pockets and stayed close beside me.

We continued our language lesson next to a large tree by the side of the street. He leaned against the tree while I rocked back and forth on my wheelchair, the front wheels sometimes lifting about three inches off the ground. He pointed to my wheelchair and then twirled his finger in circles in the air.

"Yeah. That's a good one. *Wheelchair*, right?" I pointed to my chair, and he nodded.

And then he motioned his first sentence: "Darcy no walk. Darcy wheelchair."

"Yes, Luis. That's right." I nodded.

I was so excited. It was clear to me that Luis was a lot smarter than most people gave him credit for.

"Wheelchair good," he signed with a twirling finger and a thumbs-up.

"Yeah. It is good. And tomorrow we're going to give away a bunch of 'em," I said in English.

✵ ✵ ✵

The job of passing out wheelchairs was long and hard. There were crowds of people everywhere. Some of the people were disabled. Some were family members. Others were just curious.

The different kinds of disabilities surprised me. One man crawled on the ground by squatting and then pulling his feet along with his hands. Another old woman was carried to the church in a wheelbarrow. She wore an Indian outfit and knelt in the wheelbarrow while her son pushed her along. She was no bigger than I was.

Seeing the kids made me sad. There were some with

cerebral palsy, like my friend Jessica back home. Other kids had legs that seemed to stick out in odd directions. I felt overwhelmed by so many kids my age in such rough shape. I had come down to Guatemala as the "specialist" because I was disabled. But seeing people like this made me think I was hardly disabled at all.

Pastor Rob and the others did the best they could to keep the crowd under control. The wheelchairs had been set up in a circle around the inside of the church. The crowd was to stay outside so that the workers could match them up with their wheelchairs a few at a time. Those getting a wheelchair had filled out a form and had their picture taken for the record. Workers had spent the last couple of days figuring out who should get what chair and then tagged each chair with the name of the person so that handing them out would go more quickly.

My job was to teach people how to use their new wheelchairs. I asked Monica to help me so that families could see how they should help their disabled family member. After the first five people got their wheelchairs, they came over to Monica and me. All five had the biggest smiles on their faces. I had a hard time teaching them because they were so excited.

There was a lot to learn, but they caught on

quickly. I taught them how to stop, how to turn, and how to get over bumps. Monica showed the families how to pull me up onto the curb. She also warned them to watch the road carefully to avoid small bumps and holes. "You'll dump them out onto the street if you don't watch out." Orlando translated, and everyone laughed.

Orlando and Pastor Zepeda gave each one of my students a Bible and a tract. And then they told them about Jesus and why we were giving them wheelchairs. Several nodded with smiles. "And we want you to come to church on Sunday," Pastor Zepeda said at the end.

The day went quickly for me. Though it was hard work training 50 people plus their families, it was a lot of fun. It made me feel important. The day was almost perfect, but there was one problem at the end. One very big problem.

I caught Mr. Wilcox out of the corner of my eye. He had just come through the church doorway with a very worried look on his face. Pastor Rob had called out the name of the last person to receive a wheelchair just a moment earlier. Mr. Wilcox approached Pastor Rob and whispered something in his ear. Then the two of them walked back into the church together. I could tell something was terribly wrong, so I left my post and went to the doorway. I heard them talking inside.

"But I was certain it was here," Mr. Wilcox said. "It was the last chair I tagged last night, and I remember thinking, *This little boy is certainly going to enjoy this chair.* I purposely left it for last so we could save the excitement until the end of day. You know, like saving the biggest present for last at Christmas."

Pastor Rob shook his head. Soon others were joining me at the doorway. Some went in.

"Someone must have taken it," Mr. Wilcox said. "But who would do something like that?"

"That's the problem, Señor Wilcox. Many people would," said Pastor Zepeda, who had just entered the room. "These wheelchairs are worth a lot of money, and thieves can sell them on the black market."

"Black market?" I asked.

"The black market is where stolen goods are sold at prices much higher than what things are worth, simply because the items are so rare. There's no set place for the black market. You can buy things from the sellers anywhere."

We were all upset but not as upset as the family when Pastor Zepeda told them the news. The man began to shout and point fingers. The mother cried. The boy just watched sadly and quietly.

"Please, señor, settle down," Pastor Rob urged.

"We'll try to find the wheelchair. We'll do the best we can."

The man did calm down a bit as Pastor Zepeda translated, but you could tell he was still fuming inside. I was sure he had looked forward to that wheelchair as much as his son had. There was nothing he could do, and so he picked up his son from the ground and walked away. His wife followed.

"Okay, folks," Pastor Rob announced to everyone else, "we need to track down the wheelchair. Does anyone have any clues or remember seeing someone snooping around the church?"

Everyone was quiet for a moment, thinking. Then someone in the back called out, "There was a boy here early this morning. Ah, what's his name? You know, Darcy's friend—the one who can't talk."

"Luis?" Pastor Rob asked.

"Yes, that's the boy," the man answered.

"He wouldn't do that!" I insisted. "Not Luis. Besides I was with him all day."

"But were you with him early this morning?" Pastor Rob asked.

"No. But I know he wouldn't do it. Just ask him," I pleaded and then looked around for Luis. He was usually right next to me but not this time.

"I don't see him here, Darcy," Monica said.

The crowd began looking in all directions.

"There he is!" someone shouted. We all looked down the street. There, about 100 feet from us was Luis, standing next to a garbage can. He looked at us innocently until we began to move toward him. He sensed something was wrong and, like a cornered cat, began backing away slowly. A man from our group ran ahead to catch the boy, but Luis had been a street kid too long. He took off down the street and cut into an alley faster than anyone could imagine.

"Well, I suppose that's the last we'll see of that wheelchair," said Pastor Rob.

"And that kid," added Mr. Wilcox.

I was hurting so much I couldn't speak. My throat tightened, and I could barely breathe.

"Let's pray, okay, folks?" Pastor Rob said. "Come over here, Darcy, and hold my hand. He's your special friend, and I know you must be feeling bad. Let's form a circle."

Several people prayed for the return of the wheel-chair. Others prayed for the family. A couple of people prayed for Luis. I couldn't pray though. Tears stung my eyes, and I was too choked up.

Lord, what's going on? I'm sure Luis loves You. He

wouldn't steal the wheelchair, would he? I saw Luis in my mind pointing to his heart with a smile and giving me the thumbs-up sign. *No, he wouldn't. But why, Lord? Why bring me all this way to be a missionary. I thought I had finally found one person I could share You with, and now he's gone. It seems like such a waste, Lord.*

Help me.

nine

I turned away from the circle of people after we finished praying. I couldn't face them. Even though I knew it wasn't my fault that the wheelchair had disappeared, I still felt that everyone was blaming me. No one said anything to me, and that made me feel even guiltier. Only Monica realized what I was thinking. "Listen, Darcy, you can't blame yourself for what happened. It wasn't your fault."

"I know. But it's not just that. I feel awful about Luis. I mean, what if he did do it? I just don't understand. Maybe Orlando was right. Maybe Luis did those things just because he wanted something from us."

"You can't think that way, Darcy. You were there

when we shared Christ with Luis. And you were there when he told everyone about heaven. That wasn't just made up. You know that."

Monica was firm with me. She looked me straight in the eye. "He's your friend, Darcy. He's *our* friend. You know what it means to be a friend, right?"

I nodded, tears coming to my eyes. "We've got to find him, Monica. He's out there somewhere thinking we don't like him anymore. We've got to prove that he didn't take that wheelchair."

"That's a good idea, but the Gonzalez family is expecting us for supper. How about heading out after supper to try to find him? He couldn't have gone very far, and we know where he lives."

* * *

After supper the two of us excused ourselves and headed out the door. We took along our flashlights in case it got dark. Mr. Gonzalez wasn't happy that we might be out in the dark, but we assured him we would be back soon. We just wanted to have the flashlights in case it got dark sooner than we expected.

The streets had quieted down since earlier in the day. Families sat outside on their doorsteps, enjoying the evening air and talking with one another. They watched us as we made our way down the street. It was useless calling out Luis's name. The best we could do was to look in every direction and behind buildings and cars. We saw a lot of kids and asked around a lot, but there was no sign of Luis.

"We're almost to his 'house'," I said, as we approached a small bridge. "Let's be sure not to scare him in case he's there."

We slowed our pace as we came closer. Though it was still light outside, the trees overhead and the bridge made the area dark. We turned on our flashlights. Up ahead we could see the pieces of cardboard and plywood that Luis had formed into a little hut. I could tell immediately that no one was there. The ball Luis always kept at the entrance of the hut was missing, as was the extra set of clothes.

"What have we done?" I pleaded with Monica. "Where could he go? I mean, he's already homeless!"

"Please, Darcy, stop getting upset. We'll find him. It just won't be now—that's all. You'll see. He'll show up. I'm sure of it. Let's get back to the house now. It's getting darker, and I don't think we should be out by ourselves."

⁂

That night I took out my journal as well as my flashlight. Monica had already fallen asleep, and I didn't want to turn on the overhead light. I propped myself on my side and leaned back against the wall. My Bible also lay on the bed, and I opened it first.

"So, Lord, where do I go first?" I whispered, as I held out my Bible. I thought about just flipping to any old page and pointing my finger to a spot. But then I remembered the special verse we had chosen for the trip—Proverbs 3:5-6—and decided that it was a good starting point.

"Lean not on your own understanding. . . ." I had done plenty of that on the trip, but I also remembered trusting completely in God—like when we prayed, asking God to show us how to talk with Luis about salvation.

"In all your ways acknowledge Him . . ." This was the first time in my life that I had kept God in everything. There had been lots of times when I only thought of Him when I was in trouble. On this trip I had thought of God a lot. Even the Gonzalez family helped me think about my friendship with God more. And they did it in Spanish.

"And He will direct your paths. . . ."

I looked back over those words again. That was it! That's what God wanted me to know now—and not just now but all through the entire trip. I remembered having great ideas about what I would do when I got down here and thinking I had only gotten to share Jesus with one person—a deaf person. A deaf troublemaker!

But that was God's whole idea. He knew about Luis and that I needed to help this boy. I wasn't a failure because I didn't help save hundreds of people. I was a success because I had loved just one person. That had been my job. God had brought us together. That made me all the more determined to find Luis. I just knew that not only was he innocent, but also he was to be an important part of the church here.

❊ ❊ ❊

The next day was different for me. Rather than joining the other kids down at the center of the town, I decided to hang around the church and help finish up some of the work. There were plenty of spots that needed painting, and I convinced Mr. Wilcox that I could do it, at least the bottom part.

I had been working on the side of the building in

the alley for about an hour when I noticed something out of the corner of my eye. It seemed that something or someone was watching me from the end of the alley. I turned my head slowly to the left several times, each time finding nothing.

I went back to painting. Several minutes later I heard a soft banging coming from the same place. I put down my brush and headed in that direction. Just before reaching the end of the alley, I was quickly pulled in between several large crates. When I looked up, I saw Luis staring at me with excited eyes.

"Luis!" I called out in a whisper. "They are looking for you. They say you stole a wheelchair! Did you?" I didn't have a sign for stealing, but he understood enough to get the idea.

Luis looked confused, but an idea soon came to him. "Wheelchair like yours?" he asked.

I nodded.

"Not me," he said. "I saw man with wheelchair last night. Near where I live. Not hurt like you. He walks. Maybe he took chair."

I wasn't sure whether to believe Luis so easily, but it seemed possible that it would be the same wheelchair. After all, how many wheelchairs my size that hadn't been brought by our team could there be in this town?

"Let's go." Luis grabbed my wheelchair and began pushing before I could ask more questions.

Lord, I hope he's right, I prayed silently. *This will not only help that boy, but it will also clear Luis.*

We slowed as we approached the street, not wanting to be seen. I wheeled out ahead of him to look. The coast was clear, so I quickly motioned for Luis to come. We raced across the street at full speed. Since I didn't hear any shouting behind us, I figured we had made our escape successfully.

Luis pushed me in and out of streets I had never been on before. After a while I could tell we were in a bad section of town. The people seemed rough, and the buildings were dark, without windows.

We went down one more alley and then stopped at the edge of another street. Luis pointed across the way to what appeared to be a group of one-room homes with small doors. They were made of odd-shaped concrete blocks. The area around the houses was neat, and you could tell that whoever lived there took care of things. Luis got behind me and pushed me next to a tree. He motioned for me to wait and then pointed in the direction of the huts. I followed his finger, and then I saw it.

The wheelchair that had been taken from the church! Not only that, but it was my old chair that I had given for the trip! It was like seeing an old friend in trouble, and I had to fight to keep back my tears.

"What's it doing here?" I whispered to Luis. He didn't understand, and I didn't explain. He simply motioned for me to stay there as he crept toward the chair. He crouched and walked low to the ground, moving his head back and forth on the lookout.

I watched anxiously. My heart was beating fast. I realized that if I saw any sign of trouble, I couldn't yell out a warning to Luis. He was on his own, stealing back the wheelchair!

Luis was experienced at this sort of thing, I could tell. He moved quickly from the back of one hut to the other without making any noise. At last he arrived at the wheelchair and crouched behind it. He was facing my direction now, and I saw his eyes stare back at me from between the spokes of the big wheels.

C'mon, Luis, you can do it. Oh, please, Lord, don't let him get caught. I mean, he is doing this for a good reason. After all, these people stole it from us.

Luis was within twenty feet of me when I caught

a glimpse of a man out of the corner of my eye. He had just rounded the corner of one of the huts and saw Luis immediately. He shouted and raised his arms in protest.

"Run, Luis!" I shouted and waved my arms frantically. Luis caught on and didn't bother to turn around. He ran as fast as he could toward me and then past me down the street. I wasted no time in catching up to him. Behind me were the shouts of the man and the sound of his heavy footsteps. He was gaining on us. I wanted to shout for help, but I was too panicked. The words wouldn't come out.

There was no way we could outrun him. Just then we rounded a bend in the road and saw our rescuer— a hill. A downhill! I spun my wheels all the harder to get up over the top and caught up to Luis.

"Get on!" I shouted and pointed to the chair. Luis caught on immediately and hopped on. We were off in a flash!

The man now was right behind us, but about ten yards down the hill, our chairs picked up speed, and we began to pull away from him. The wind and sun in our faces and the thrill of tricking a thief was exciting. I whooped and hollered all the way down. Luis laughed in his funny sort of way, looking back every once in a while to be sure we were safe. We were. At the bottom of the hill we took a side street in the direction of the church.

When we arrived, a big crowd of the workers and host families were out front, standing back to admire the work on the church. Someone had finished my job in the alley while I was gone, and the workers had come down off the roof. I saw Pastor Rob and Mr. Wilcox coming out of the church.

"Pastor Rob!" I called out. "Look over here. Look what we've got!" I said excitedly. Luis and I both wheeled our way closer, sitting proudly in our two wheelchairs.

"Where in the world—" Mr. Wilcox stopped in mid-sentence.

"Isn't it cool?" I said. "Luis got it back for us. He took me to the other side of town."

"But how? Where?"

"He . . ." Now I realized just what we had done, and I got a lump in my throat. I started breathing heavily, and my face flushed. This was going to be hard to explain. "He—he, ah. . . . Well, you see, Luis—Luis and I kinda like—" Pastor Rob wasn't the only one listening by this time after all my stops and starts. There were three or four faces with lots of questions.

"We stole it back," I finally blurted out.

"You stole it? From whom? Where?"

"It was somewhere on the other side of town, up on the hill."

Orlando had joined us. "I know that place. Pretty tough people live there. Some say they steal things and do bad business for the black market. One of them probably took the chair from us yesterday and didn't have a chance to sell it yet."

Pastor Rob walked over to Luis. "Young man," he said, "I'm sorry. I'm sure you know most of us thought you stole it. That was wrong for us to do. I hope you'll forgive us."

Pastor Zepeda and the rest of the church and our team had gathered around us. Luis was nervous again, but our smiles kept him from running this time.

"You've done good, Luis," I said. I pointed to him and gave him a thumbs-up sign. He signed it back to me. And then Luis did something that won everyone's hearts. He reached into his pocket and pulled out a small brown bag. He handed it to Pastor Zepeda.

Pastor Zepeda opened the bag and looked inside. His eyes seemed to pop out of his head. He reached into the bag and pulled out a wad of money—pesos.

"Where did you get this?" I asked Luis. I held out my hands to my side and pointed to the money.

Luis put his head down, realizing what I was asking. "Luis bad," he signed.

"It must be money he's stolen as a street kid," Orlando said. "He probably just kept saving it."

"And now he's giving it to the church, I think," I said. "Money to church?" I motioned to Luis. He nodded yes.

The crowd applauded. If anyone had needed convincing that Luis was a changed boy, this latest action did the trick. Luis was a new boy. He was a Christian. And he was a part of this little church.

Ten

The scene outside the church looked like a big party. Luis got lots of hugs and handshakes from everyone. He was not used to so much attention from so many people, and so he stood in quiet wonder at it all. He had probably never had as many hugs in his entire lifetime as he received during those few minutes!

"I think he's found some friends, Darcy," Pastor Rob said. "And we have you and Monica to thank for sticking by this young fellow."

"It wasn't us really," I said, uncomfortable with the compliment but still liking it. "God had to tell him the things we were trying to say."

"Yeah," Monica added. "It certainly wasn't us.

People who know sign language would probably laugh at us if they watched the kinds of signs we used for words."

Pastor Rob gave us the thumbs-up sign as he headed for his host family's house. It was getting late, and we could see several of the other team members making their way with their host families back to their homes. It was getting near suppertime. It was also our last night in the town, which meant everyone had a lot of packing to do.

I turned toward Luis who by this time was standing alone, watching the rest of the well-wishers make their way down the street. He turned and looked at me with a "what-now" kind of look on his face. He wanted more of what he had just gotten, and I could tell he didn't want to go back to his shack.

Monica was looking at Luis as well. "Darcy, what's he going to do? We can't just leave him here. That would be cruel."

Luis made his way over to us. We began to whisper instinctively. "I wonder if he could come home with us for supper tonight," I said. "You and I could each share our food with him."

"Great idea. But how? It's not our house."

We were puzzled as to what to do and did our

best to ignore Luis. Fortunately we weren't the only ones who had been thinking about him. So had our host family. "Luis eat at our house tonight," Mr. Gonzalez said to Monica and me in English, pointing at Luis.

"Did you get that, Luis?" I asked excitedly. I motioned with my hands as if shoveling food into my mouth, pointed at Luis, and then pointed at Mr. Gonzalez.

Luis understood instantly and was genuinely pleased. He jumped back and forth sideways, as if he were on a pogo stick.

"Come." Mr. Gonzalez motioned to Luis and took the boy's hand in his own large hand. We all made our way down the street for supper and what was to be a new beginning for Luis.

Our supper was different that night. Rather than the noisy chatter of English and Spanish, we all seemed caught up in Luis's quiet world, and so we barely spoke. Often we motioned when we wanted something or when we wanted to ask a question. After a while we got to laughing at our obvious attempts to avoid speaking. It would have been simple enough to ask Monica to get me a napkin, but I motioned it instead. It took me five minutes to explain what I wanted in between laughs that made my side ache.

"We pray now," Mr. Gonzalez said as we finished the meal. "We thank God for Luis and pray for him."

We all bowed our heads. Luis watched us at first, but then he too bowed his head, folding his hands like the two little girls who sat next to him. I don't know what Mr. Gonzalez prayed, but when we opened our eyes, we knew that both he and his wife were feeling emotional. I didn't ask why. I only hoped it was for good reasons.

As we all left the table, Luis made his way to the front door. He motioned to me that he was leaving. He also motioned to Mrs. Gonzalez that his stomach felt good and smiled.

"Stop," Mr. Gonzalez said in Spanish. He motioned for Luis to come back into the room.

"Tell him he stay here. Sleep here in house," Mr. Gonzalez told Monica and me. "Tell him."

"Luis," I motioned to him, "you stay here tonight." I pointed to him and then made the sign for sleeping. I pointed to the couch in the room.

Luis didn't catch on at first, and so Monica gave it a try. She took him by the hand and pointed to the couch and then to him. "Stay here tonight," she said out loud.

Luis's eyes got big and wide. He couldn't believe it and so made his way again to the door.

"No, no." I pulled him back. "You're sleeping here tonight."

The entire Gonzalez family smiled and waited, as if Luis would give them an answer out loud. He slowly nodded his head instead. He would have smiled, I'm sure, but it was too unbelievable for him.

We played some games—"Rocks, Scissors, and Paper," charades, and a card game called Uno. Luis joined us in every game and did quite well. The girls giggled at his mistakes, but he didn't seem to mind a bit. At around eight o'clock, Monica and I headed for bed.

"We have to pack our things," we said. "Good night, Luis. Good night, girls."

"Thank you for letting Luis spend the night," I told Mrs. Gonzalez. I pointed to Luis, and she understood. We all said good night. Monica and I went to our room.

"Well, this is it," I said as we got undressed. "By tomorrow night we'll be in our own beds back home."

"That'll be a relief," Monica said. "It's been fun here, but I could sure use a comfortable mattress."

"And a hot shower!" I added. "But I'm a bit sad too. I feel like we just got here, and now we're leaving."

"I know what you mean. We got a lot done for the church, but there are a lot of things that still need to be done."

"Like there's something not quite finished, right?" I asked.

"Uh huh. But I can't figure out what it is. Just a funny feeling."

We climbed into our beds, and Monica turned off the light. The moon made its presence known in the room. I could hear the three girls giggling next door in their room. It was quiet out in the living room where I pictured Luis getting comfortable on something soft for a change.

Lord, what happens now? What's Luis going to do? We helped out as best we could, but now what? I see that You had a plan for me on this trip, but now that Luis is in Your family, what happens to him? Will he still be a street kid? The only way he can get money for food would be to steal, and he won't do that. At least I hope he won't. . . .

I lay awake trying to think of ways to help him— sending him money each month from America, taking him with us—but nothing seemed quite right. I drifted off into a troubled sleep thinking about a little boy who couldn't hear or talk.

Our team gathered around the bus the next day.

All the bags were piled up outside the back of the bus. Several people were taking pictures of their host families and getting last-minute shots of the church building. The street in front of the church was a festive place as many people from the town gathered around to say good-bye to us.

We stood near the front door of the bus. The Gonzalez family stood together nearby. Luis stood next to me, holding my hand and obviously worried. He knew what was happening, and I read the fear on his face.

"Don't worry, Luis," I said. I didn't really feel hopeful, but I didn't know what else to say. I made a thumbs-up sign for him and smiled weakly. *He can tell I'm faking it!*

"Have you thought of any ideas, Monica?" I asked.

"Not one. I don't know what we can do to help. I'm going to give him money from my wallet, but it won't go very far."

We stood in silence until Mr. Gonzalez stepped forward. "Darcy. Monica. I tell you something. Need Mr. Rick."

I called over to Rick, "Can you help us?"

Rick came over, and I motioned to Mr. Gonzalez

and said, "He wants to tell us something. Probably an official good-bye or something."

Rick and Mr. Gonzalez got into a long discussion. Rick asked a lot of questions. Mr. Gonzalez seemed intent on convincing Rick about something, and Rick seemed not to believe him. I heard Luis's name mentioned every once in while and began to worry that perhaps he had done something wrong. I tried to interrupt Rick to get him to translate, but he ignored me. I finally yanked on his shirt sleeve.

"What's going on?"

He turned to me with a smile. "You're not going to believe this. I'm not so sure I've got it right, but I'm going to get Pastor Rob and Pastor Zepeda."

The two pastors came, and within a minute or so our little good-bye circle grew to a good-sized group.

"Let me tell you what's happening," Rick said. "Pastor Zepeda, Pastor Rob, and Mr. Gonzalez are talking about Luis."

"Yeah. We figured that. What are they saying?" Monica asked.

"Well, it seems the Gonzalez family wants Luis to come and stay with them. They are talking with Pastor Zepeda to see if he would help them make that legal."

"Make what legal?" I asked.

"You know, adopting him. Mr. and Mrs. Gonzalez want Luis to be their son!"

I felt like I was either hearing a giant fireworks display going off with a live band in the background or feeling thunder—the kind that goes right to your bones on a hot summer night. The words "Mr. and Mrs. Gonzalez want Luis to be their son!" was like a shout from God telling me that He cared not only about Luis, but also about me and about what I cared about. I turned to Monica with tears in my eyes. We hugged each other and held on tight.

"Rick," I finally said, "we want to tell Luis, but are you sure? Does Pastor Zepeda think it will work?"

"Oh yeah. No problem. They say it's simple for such a thing to happen. The townspeople will be happy to see the adoption take place. As far as they're concerned, it will mean one less thief on the street."

I turned to Luis as the reality sank in. "Luis," I said, "You. The Gonzalez family. Together." I motioned the best I could. It was hard to explain, so I took him over to where Mr. and Mrs. Gonzalez were talking with the pastors. I grabbed his hand and placed it on Mr. Gonzalez's arm. Then I hugged myself and then pointed to Luis and to Mr. Gonzalez. Luis didn't understand.

"I tell him," Mr. Gonzalez said. With that he held Luis at arms' length and said, "I love you," in Spanish. Luis didn't respond, but Mr. Gonzalez then wrapped Luis in his arms and hugged him tightly. Then he reached for his wife and three girls, and all joined in a big group hug.

The message was clear to Luis at last. He couldn't help but know that he now had a family—a family just for him. All his days of sleeping in his shack, of stealing, of going without food, of being lonely were over. He belonged to Jesus. And now he belonged to people who wanted to spend the rest of their lives with him. He held on tightly to Mr. Gonzalez even after the family loosened their hug.

We stood in silence, several of us crying for joy, until we heard Mr. Wilcox yell out, "All aboard, everyone. We've got to get to the airport." Walking over to us, he said, "And you know what that means, Darcy. You're on first."

"Well, this is it," I said, turning to Luis. "I'm going home to my family. You've got yours now. I'll always remember you. And I'll pray for you."

I took my friendship bracelet off. "Here, Luis. You take this." I put it in his hands. "Share the story about Jesus with someone."

Luis took it from me and gave me a long, hard hug. He did the same to Monica.

"I'll send you a letter," Monica said. "I know you'll learn how to read real soon. I just know it."

The ride to the airport was even wilder and more lively than the ride out to the town. Everyone traded stories of their adventures and began lots of sentences with "Do you remember when we . . . ?"

I turned to look out the window and tuned out the noise around me. I watched the green hills in the distance and thought about all that had happened. My dreams of turning Guatemala upside down for God and being a disability specialist seemed silly. I didn't speak to huge crowds of people. I didn't lead a bunch of disabled people to do something special with their wheelchairs. But I knew inside that God had sent me to Guatemala because of one boy named Luis. We had crossed paths because God wanted it that way.

I looked back at Monica who sat next to me. She was listening to a conversation in front of her but turned when she sensed I was looking at her.

"I love you," I said.

"Same here. I'm glad we're sisters. I'll hang out with you in any part of the world any day."

We had left our quiet town of nice lawns and

white fences, and two weeks later we were returning as different people. Different, because Monica and I were not just sisters. We had become friends. And we had grown up quickly—grown up just in time to face the days ahead when there would be new challenges and when we would not be together often. The thought scared me a little, but then I remembered that "God will direct our paths."